The Secret

by

Kathi Daley

This book is dedicated to my beautiful niece Abby, who asked Aunt Kathi for a series geared toward teens and got one.

I also want to thank the very talented Jessica Fischer for the cover art.

And, of course, thanks to the readers and bloggers in my life who make doing what I do possible.

And, as always, love and thanks to my sister Christy for her time, encouragement, and unwavering support. I also want to thank Carrie, Cristin, Brennen, and Danny for the Facebook shares, Randy Ladenheim-Gil for the editing, and, last but not least, my super-husband Ken for allowing me time to write by taking care of everything else.

Books by Kathi Daley

Come for the murder, stay for the romance.

Buy them on Amazon today.

Zoe Donovan Cozy Mystery:

Halloween Hijinks
The Trouble With Turkeys
Christmas Crazy
Cupid's Curse
Big Bunny Bump-off
Beach Blanket Barbie
Maui Madness
Derby Divas
Haunted Hamlet
Turkeys, Tuxes, and Tabbies
Christmas Cozy
Alaskan Alliance
Matrimony Meltdown – *April 2015*
Soul Surrender – *May 2015*
Heavenly Honeymoon – *June 2015*

Zoe Donovan Cookbook

Ashton Falls Cozy Cookbook

Paradise Lake Cozy Mystery:

Pumpkins in Paradise
Snowmen in Paradise
Bikinis in Paradise
Christmas in Paradise
Puppies in Paradise

Whales and Tails Cozy Mystery:

Romeow and Juliet
The Mad Catter
Grimm's Furry Tail

Seacliff High Mystery Series:

The Secret
The Curse – May 2015
The Relic – July 2015

Road to Christmas Romance:

Road to Christmas Past

Note to the reader:

I initially wrote this book over eight years ago, long before I wrote the cozy mystery series I currently publish. It has been sitting on my computer all this time, gathering dust (metaphorically). I have had several fans ask me to write a series geared toward a teen audience, so I decided to dust off the Seacliff High series and publish it.

Over the years I've borrowed a concept or two from this unpublished series and used them in my other books. I'm mentioning this in case the more observant among you recognize certain themes. I decided to publish these books as they were written, so please bear with any similarities between these books and concepts explored in my other series.

I hope you enjoy visiting Cutter's Cove. This series has always been near and dear to my heart.

Chapter 1

Sunday, September 3, 2006

Though he'd been dead for nearly four years, he stood at the end of the bed, silhouetted in the darkness. His features were faint, like a blurry watercolor that hinted at images not clearly defined. Eyes that were felt more than seen beckoned her toward him. Alyson didn't believe in ghosts, but somehow she wasn't at all surprised to find him standing there. She'd felt his presence for days, watching her, judging her, waiting to make his presence known at just the right time. He looked just like she'd pictured him, gnarled and wrinkled, his back curved with age.

"Barkley?"

The image faded into the darkness. Alyson rolled over onto her side and switched on the bedside lamp. Nothing. Old houses tended to be temperamental and unpredictable. This wasn't the first time the electricity had failed.

Fumbling around for some matches, she lit the candle she kept for just such occasions. The flickering light illuminated the room, casting eerie shadows on the faded wallpaper. A Prada wrap dress tossed haphazardly across a three-legged chair came alive as the breeze from the cracked window caused it to flutter and sway. An empty coatrack, abandoned by a previous resident, reached out to her, arms broken and splintered like a frail old man.

Alyson slipped out of bed and wrapped a white silk robe around her body. She curled her toes against the cold as she made her way across the scuffed wooden floor, pausing to listen, as she turned the knob on her battered door and opened it just an inch.

Peering into the inky darkness, she searched for any sign of her nocturnal guest.

"Barkley? Are you out here?"

Taking a deep breath, she listened. A steady ticktock as the grandfather clock at the end of the hallway marked off the minutes. The muffled sound of waves crashing on the rocky shoreline beyond the thick walls of the ancient house. The thundering of her own heartbeat as she slowly released the breath she'd been holding. She looked toward the sanctuary of her bed, then opened the door an inch further. A sliver of light from the third-floor window pierced the darkness, casting shadows that appeared to waltz across the landing.

Opening the door enough to squeeze through, she crept into the hallway, shining the light from her candle toward the narrow staircase. Glancing toward the haven of her mother's closed door at the other end of the hall, she edged toward the stairs with her back to the wall.

"Barkley?" she breathed.

She paused and listened with each step she took. One, two, three, four, remember to breathe, only nine stairs more. Stepping over the third stair from the top, which tended to creak under your weight, she reached the landing and looked around. Four doors, all closed. Three led to bedrooms, one to a bath. Glancing up the staircase, which continued toward the fourth-floor attic, she hesitated. The attic had been securely locked ever since she and her mother had moved in three weeks earlier. They'd tried to open it several times, but it had obviously become solidly rusted over the years, like a weathered seal on an ancient tomb. The handyman had informed them that the door would need to be removed; sometimes old locks became frozen with age.

Taking a step toward the first closed door, she looked again toward the impenetrable entrance at the top of the rickety stairs. It beckoned her to try once again. It wasn't rational; rusted locks don't suddenly free themselves to reveal their treasures. Alyson turned and stepped cautiously onto the first wobbly stair leading to the attic. She'd always been more curious than rational, and more often than not that had landed her in trouble.

The stairs were uneven and decaying; one wrong step and . . . Alyson didn't want to think about that. She wondered about residents past. Had anyone stumbled on them? Maybe even fallen? A trip down the steep wooden stairs wouldn't be pleasant at all. Gripping the wooden railing tighter, she stepped over a broken floorboard and scampered safely onto the fourth-floor landing.

Pausing in front of the door, she slowly turned the knob. The door opened effortlessly, groaning under the strain of years without movement. The windowless room, damp and musty with age, echoed the silent voices of lives past and secrets long buried. Cobwebs hung from the ceiling, their intricate patterns crisscrossing across the doorway. Standing on her tiptoes, she tried to peer over the boxes and furniture piled from floor to ceiling as far back as her limited view could discern. She wondered about the owners of the long-forgotten cache, the generations of men, women, and children who had once stored their most precious memories and prized possessions within these very walls.

Barkley had led her here; she felt it in her gut. Somewhere among the discarded remnants of lives past was a secret he wanted her to find. Tiffany would love this—a mystery to solve. Tiffany had always been the more adventurous of the two of them. Too bad she was dead.

Alyson closed the door, being careful not to trip the rusty lock. Barkley's secret would have to wait. Tonight she needed her sleep. Tomorrow her new life would officially begin. A life that would be totally different from everything she had ever known. Alyson smiled as she pulled her robe more tightly around her shivering body and started back down the stairs. Ghosts and hidden secrets; who would have thought that her life could get any crazier than it already was? Her court-appointed shrink would have had a field day with this.

Chapter 2

"Breakfast is almost ready," Mom called from the bottom of the stairs.

"Coming." Alyson pulled on a well-worn pair of jeans and a royal blue cashmere sweater she'd picked up at Barneys's after-holiday clearance last year. She gave herself a once-over in the full-length mirror, which she'd taped haphazardly to the door just two days before. "It'll have to do."

Scooping up the piles of clothes she tried on and then discarded, she tossed them on the hand-me-down bed she'd covered with silk designer sheets. It hadn't been too long ago that she'd known exactly what to wear, the perfect attire for every occasion. She'd been a trendsetter teens all over the city looked to for the latest thing.

The problem was her clothes were all wrong for a small rural high school, where the average household income for an entire month approximated the cost of a single pair of her shoes. In her old life she'd always set the fashion trends; now all she wanted to do was fit in.

Pulling her long blond hair into a neat ponytail that fell halfway down her back, she slipped her perfectly pedicured feet into a pair of strappy sandals and deemed herself ready for whatever Seacliff High School had to throw at her. Grabbing her cropped leather jacket and leather handbag from the hook on the back of the door, she took one last look around the room. Faded wallpaper, scuffed hardwood floor, discarded furniture, and tens of thousands of dollars' worth of designer clothes. The room seemed to perfectly represent the disjointed and fractured reality that her life had become, where nothing seemed to fit and everything felt like a lie. Maybe if she helped Barkley find his peace she'd find her own. She closed the door to her ransacked room and headed down the narrow stairs toward the kitchen below.

"So, are you ready for your first day at your new school?" her mom questioned as she walked into the kitchen.

Alyson poured herself a glass of orange juice and began buttering a piece of toast without responding. "I'm sure the curriculum isn't what you're used to. Are you sure you don't want me to look into getting you into that private girls' school up the coast? I could ask Donovan to make some discreet inquiries." Donovan had become her handler five months earlier, when Alyson and her mother had been placed in witness protection. He was the only person in the entire world besides the two of them who knew where they were or who they had become.

"Amanda Parker, heiress to millions, went to a private girls' school." Alyson walked over to the table and plopped a bite of scrambled egg into her mouth.

"Alyson Prescott," she continued, "a totally normal girl, living a totally normal life, in a totally normal small town, would never be able to afford such a luxury. Besides, public school might be fun. I've always wondered what it would be like to have access to a smorgasbord of male hunks right in my very own classroom."

"You're right. I guess I just need to get use to all the changes."

"Have you talked to Donovan lately?"

"Yesterday. They've had a few new leads, but nothing significant. He thinks we're safe for now, but, as usual, he warned us to be careful."

"And Dad?"

"He didn't say, but I'm sure he's fine. There was an article about him in *Society* magazine a few weeks ago. It seems that ever since my death he's become the most eligible widower in New York."

"I'm sorry. I know this must be hard for you."

"Go brush your teeth and I'll give you a ride to school. Can't be late on the very first day."

The trip into town had become a daily pilgrimage for Cutter's Cove's newest residents. Ever since Alyson and her mom had moved to Cutter's Cove, Oregon, three weeks ago, they'd been working around the clock to make the dilapidated old house they'd bought somewhat livable. After at least twenty trips to the hardware store, hundreds of hours of elbow grease, and a little ingenuity, they'd managed to make two of the bedrooms, a bathroom, and the kitchen marginally functional. Of course, it would require months of hard work and countless additional trips to the hardware store before the old house would be truly habitable. They'd looked at a few more practical houses when they first got to town, but it was love at first sight when they spotted the large, well-lived-in house sitting empty on the edge of a rocky cliff overlooking the Pacific Ocean.

"Here we are," Mom announced as she pulled into the parking lot of the local high school. "Are you nervous?"

Alyson crossed the first two fingers of her left hand. "Not really."

"I'll pick you up at three. Maybe we could drive in to Portland, have dinner, and do some shopping. I'd like to avoid a reoccurrence of the tornado that hit your room this morning."

"Actually," Alyson hesitated, "I'm hoping we can go down to the DMV after school to make an appointment for me to take my driving test. I know, I know," she held up her hand to ward off her mother's objections, "after what happened, you want me to wait. But I have waited, four whole months; I'm ready. I've taken the classes, watched the gory movies, and studied the Oregon Drivers Handbook. I'll probably be the only junior who doesn't drive. Please—I want to fit in."

"What I was going to say, if I'd been allowed to speak, is that I agree with you. It's time for you to get on with your life, and I'd be glad to take you to the DMV after school. Shopping can wait for another day."

"Thanks, Mom. I love you." Alyson hugged her mom and opened the car door. Getting out, she paused to look around. "Wish me friends."

The school was old and run-down. The majority of the town's citizens worked in the fishing or tourism industries, and walls in need of painting and floors that didn't quite shine told a story of years of tight budgets. The school was a lifetime away from the exclusive private school she'd attended in New

York, but with its homey show of school spirit, as evidenced by the brightly painted posters filling every available wall space, it felt just right.

Alyson pulled out her schedule and tried to figure out which of the three main halls she should take to find her first class, AP Chemistry. Her paperwork said the class was being held in room B3, so she headed down the middle hall, assuming wings A, B, and C would probably fall in some type of order, with B conveniently ending up in the middle. The room was right where she expected to find it, third door down in the identified B wing. She paused outside and looked in through the small window in the door. Picking out just the right seat was possibly the most important thing you did on your first day at a new school. For one thing, the people you sat closest to had the highest new friend potential. For another, this being a science class, the person you sat next to would probably end up being your lab partner for the semester. She just needed to find a smart-looking but friendly candidate who didn't already have a tablemate.

There appeared to be about a dozen students in the class. Most of the students were already paired up, including one simply gorgeous football player type sitting next to an equally gorgeous cheerleader type. Too bad.

Sitting right in front of the superhunk, a girl with long red pigtails laughed at something he said. Alyson immediately liked her friendly smile and completely outrageous outfit. Now *there* was a girl who wasn't afraid to dress to the beat of her own drummer. She appeared confident and assured, comfortable in her own skin, a unique quality in the face of the abject conformity most students adhered to. Plus, she appeared to be friends with superhunk, which earned her bonus points, because getting an introduction seemed highly likely.

Making up her mind, she opened the door and, taking a deep breath for courage, ventured into the room.

"Is this stool taken?" she asked the red-haired girl as she approached.

"No, have a seat. Are you new around here? I haven't seen you around before, and in a town this size everyone pretty much knows everyone else."

"I'm Alyson Prescott. I moved here from—" she crossed her fingers in her lap—"Minnesota. Three weeks ago."

"Delighted to meet you, Alyson Prescott from Minnesota. My name is Makenzie Reynolds, Mac for short, and this pretty boy behind me is Trevor Johnson."

"Glad to have you aboard." Trevor smiled.

"Uh-hum." The dark-haired girl sitting next to Trevor cleared her throat.

"Oh, this is Chelsea Green," Mac added less enthusiastically.

"Charmed, I'm sure." Chelsea glared at Alyson with cold eyes, obviously less enthusiastic than the other two to have a new girl in town.

"I've never been to Minnesota, but I hear it's cold. Is it cold? I'm sure it's cold."

"Mac, you're rambling." Trevor tossed a paper football at her. "Being new to the area, I'm sure you'll need someone to show you around. I'm a great tour guide. I'd be happy to introduce you to Cutter's Cove's finer sights any time. Say after school?"

"You're busy." Chelsea glared at Alyson, then turned her brightest smile on Trevor. "Remember, you promised to help me with the posters for the dance. Mac can show her around."

"Actually, I'm supposed to go somewhere with my mom after school, but thanks anyway. Maybe another time?"

The teacher walked in, and Alyson turned around to give him her full attention.

"Good morning, class," the thin man with wire-rimmed glasses greeted them. "My name is Mr. Harris. This is Advance Placement Chemistry. I assume everyone is in the right place?"

There were general murmurs of acknowledgment from around the room.

"Good, then let's get started. The person you're sitting next to will be your lab partner for the semester."

Alyson noticed Chelsea's satisfied smile and Trevor's glare at Mac, who grimaced apologetically to Trevor. All might not be as it at first appeared. Maybe Trevor and Chelsea weren't a couple, as Alyson had first assumed. In fact, it seemed Trevor had planned on partnering up with Mac. Interesting.

"Those of you sitting alone at a table should pair up with a partner." Mr. Harris started writing on the blackboard. "The plan for today is simply to get to know one another and go over the quite extensive syllabus for the semester. Tomorrow, though, you should plan on digging in and getting right to the meat of things. This is an AP class, so it won't be easy. I expect excellence from each and every one of you. If you didn't come to this class to work harder than you ever have before, there's a basic junior-level class going on right next door. I'd be happy to sign transfer papers for anyone who's not really serious about science."

Mr. Harris paused, as if giving everyone a chance to think over his offer. Alyson liked him already. She had been concerned that after ten years of private school she wouldn't be challenged in a small public school like Seacliff. She noticed Mac's enthusiastic smile at Mr. Harris's speech. Things were definitely looking up.

The class passed quickly, with Mr. Harris talking at marathon speed the entire hour. Alyson wondered how he could keep up the pace without ever seeming to stop to breathe, but the syllabus seemed both interesting and challenging and Alyson couldn't wait to get started.

"Do you know where room A6 is?" Alyson asked Mac after class. She'd figured out corridor B would fall in the middle but wasn't sure if the halls were labeled left to right or vice versa.

"Sure; in fact, I'm headed there myself. You can walk with me."

"You have AP English next period?"

Back-to-back classes together; Alyson smiled to herself. What a break. She might even be able to score an invitation to sit at Mac's table at lunch, with a double exposure opportunity.

"Yeah. You'll find a lot of familiar faces in your AP classes because the school only offers one section of each subject."

"I have AP Calculus third period then AP U.S. history fourth," Alyson added. "Looks like we can be study buddies."

This was getting better and better.

"So Trevor and Chelsea. Are they a couple?" Alyson inquired.

Mac laughed. "In the fantasy that's in Chelsea's mind maybe, but otherwise, no way. Trevor barely tolerates her. He's just too nice to tell her to buzz off."

"So, does he have a girl?"

"Why? You interested."

"No," Alyson denied quickly. "I just met him. I'm just curious."

"Guess you'll have to get to know him a little better and ask him yourself."

Alyson stuck her tongue out at Mac in a very unjuniorlike manner, and then turned to give her attention to the teacher who had just walked in. She could hear Mac giggle beside her. She really liked this girl. Hopefully the feeling was mutual. She would be happy to make any new friends on the first day of her new life, but one as easygoing and unpretentious as Mac was an added bonus.

By the time lunch came around, it was assumed by all that Alyson would be joining Mac and Trevor at their table. The lunchroom was crowded, with long cafeteria tables and a menu offering burgers and sandwiches. Alyson chose a salad and a diet soda from the limited offerings and turned to join her friends.

"So, you don't happen to have PE followed by computer lab?" Alyson asked Mac as she maneuvered herself onto the bench beside her.

"No, I actually go off campus for a special program offered by a software company out of Portland. It counts as both high school and college credit, plus it's miles more advanced and tons more interesting than anything this place could offer."

"Mac's a ·computer savant," Trevor added playfully. "In fact, I've often wondered if she has computer chips implanted where her brain is supposed to be."

"Very funny." Mac kicked Trevor under the table.

"So we have a real computer genius in our midst." Alyson took a bite of her salad. "I can barely manage to surf the Web without getting all flubbed up. I'd love to get some one-on-one instruction from someone who knows all the tricks."

"Sure, anytime," Mac offered.

"How about you, Trevor?" Alyson asked. "Any special talents I should know about?"

"He's probably the best jock in the county and he's got the prettiest face in the whole state. Don't you, pretty boy?" Mac teased.

"Knock it off, Mac," Trevor complained. "You know I hate it when you call me that."

"I just call 'em as I see 'em."

"I should have punched you out in the first grade when you first started calling me that. Maybe I could have ended it right then and there."

"You know you'd never hit me." Mac threw a French fry at Trevor's head. "You love me too much. Besides, I'd have kicked your butt in the first grade and we both know it."

Alyson watched the playful banter and wondered if maybe the two of them were a couple after all. Of course they seemed more like squabbling siblings than hot and steamy lovers, but who knew? Love was strange and could be expressed in a lot of different ways.

After lunch Alyson went off to PE, where the only familiar face was Chelsea's, and she didn't acknowledge her, and then computer lab, where she recognized no one. She'd have to work on making a friend in PE; it was always good to have an ally when people were throwing balls of one sort or another at you. Computer lab was a self-study program, so she actually preferred to go it alone. If she got her work done early she could surf the Web and keep an eye on the goings-on back home in New York without her mother worrying that somehow someone would track her down through the maze that was the World Wide Web.

Chapter 3

"I'll pick you up after school for your appointment at the DMV," Mom said the next morning as she slid light and fluffy blueberry pancakes onto Alyson's plate.

"I hope there are no problems with my new birth certificate. This is the first time we've really tried it out."

"I'm sure it will be fine. Donovan knows what he's doing. We didn't have any trouble enrolling you in school."

"Yeah, I guess."

Alyson poured warm syrup over the mound of pancakes in front of her and took a huge bite. "You make the best pancakes." Alyson chewed slowly to fully savor the flavor. "Truly, if you ever get tired of the art world, you could always become a chef."

"I appreciate the compliment, but I love painting and I can't wait to get back to it. It's been so long," she added a little sadly. "Now that you've somehow managed to miraculously open the rusted lock, how about helping me clean out the attic this weekend so I can set up my studio? I have a contractor coming over this morning to fix the stairs."

"Sure, Mom, I'd love to help. There certainly is a lot of stuff packed up there. Do you ever wonder why the previous owner left so much behind?"

"The Realtor mentioned that Barkley Cutter lived here his entire life until he died four years ago. The place has been empty ever since."

"But what about his heirs?" Alyson questioned.

"I'm not really sure. I bought the house from some type of trust. Actually," Mom elaborated, "I offered cash, so they didn't ask a lot of questions, and I wanted to keep things as simple and quiet as possible, so I didn't ask a lot of questions either."

"It'd be kind of neat to learn the history of the place. I mean, it's really old, probably from the nineteenth century. And it must have been fabulous at one point—three stories of living space, a huge attic, and a dark and dank but fairly large cellar. And you can't beat the view." Alyson looked out the large picture window to the blue waters of the ocean beyond.

"Maybe you could dig up some information on the house at the local historical society. That is, if this town even has one," Mom suggested. "If not, maybe the local library."

"I think I'll do that. Maybe I'll ask around. The kids I met yesterday seemed like they've lived here a long time, so they probably know at least a little bit about the place." Alyson looked toward the clock above the brand-new stove that had been installed two weeks earlier. "Right now," she added, taking her dishes to the sink, "I'd better get going or I'll be late for school."

"I'll get my coat," Mom said, getting up from her chair.

Mac waved enthusiastically as Alyson walked in the classroom for first period. Alyson felt an immediate affection for this quirky little town and its friendly residents. She'd lived in New York her entire life, and had many good friends there, but she'd never received quite as warm a welcome as she had from someone she'd met only the day before.

"We were talking about the Kickoff to Football Season dance in two weeks," Mac began to speak as soon as Alyson got within hearing range. "You're going to come, aren't you?"

Alyson sat her new backpack on the table in front of her and climbed onto the tall stool.

"You simply have to," Mac added without giving Alyson a chance to answer. "Our first home game will be on Friday night, followed by the annual bonfire out at Cutter's Field." Mac squirmed on her seat, completely caught up in the enthusiasm of the moment. "Then, on Saturday, there's a parade and a pancake breakfast in the morning and a dance that night."

"Boy, you people really love your football, don't you?" Alyson observed.

"Yeah, I guess you could say this is a football town." Mac flipped one of her long braids over the shoulder of her Seacliff Pirates sweatshirt. "So how about it? You'll come, won't you?"

"I'd love to. I wouldn't miss it for the world." Alyson was surprised to find she really meant it. Who'd have thought? High school football, and she felt excited at the prospect.

"Trevor is the best quarterback in the state," Chelsea boasted, hugging his arm possessively.

"We're really going to kick some butt this year," Mac agreed. "We might even make state finals."

"It's about time the cheerleaders get the exposure they deserve. After two years of cheering for a lackluster team, we deserve to go to state."

"Chelsea," Mac reasoned, "don't you think that maybe it's the players and not the cheerleaders who deserve a little recognition?"

"If they do their job I guess we'll all get what we want."

"Class, can I have your attention?" Mr. Harris spoke from the front of the room.

"We'll talk more at lunch," Mac whispered to Alyson as she turned to give the teacher her full attention.

The dining selections hadn't improved from the day before, so Alyson selected a couple of pieces of fruit and went to join Mac, Trevor, and Chelsea, who were already seated at a table by the window.

"The menu for the lunchroom could use a serious makeover," Alyson complained, setting her selections on the table next to Mac's.

"Tell me about it," Chelsea agreed. "This place is definitely not diet friendly. I usually just bring a protein bar to school instead of ruining my diet with the crap they serve here."

"Your figure is fine," Trevor responded. "I don't know why you girls are so diet crazy anyway."

"Keeping an absolutely perfect figure like this takes work," Chelsea explained. "But thanks for noticing," she added, cuddling closer to the hunk sitting next to her. "Besides, diet is only part of it. There's exercise, and massage, and of course there's always . . ."

"So, Alyson," Mac interrupted, "are you doing anything this weekend? I thought we could go to the Cannery on Friday night, and then maybe I could show you around a little on Saturday. Not that there's much to see, but I figured being new and all, you probably don't know the better places to shop."

"Sounds like fun, but I promised my mom I'd help her clean out the attic on Saturday. She likes to paint and she wants to use the space as a studio. I'd love to do something on Friday night, though."

"You just moved here and you already need to clean out your attic?" Trevor dipped one of his big, greasy onion rings in a mound of ketchup.

"Actually, we bought a bit of a fixer-upper and the previous owner left all of his personal stuff behind. It's mostly junk, but the attic is packed floor to ceiling."

"Why'd the previous owner leave his stuff when he moved?" Chelsea asked.

"He didn't move. He died." Alyson took a bite of her apple.

"You didn't buy the old Cutter place, did you?" Trevor wiped a dollop of ketchup from his chin.

"Yeah, that's the one."

"Man, that place is a dump." Trevor took a huge bite of his hamburger, chewed twice, and then swallowed. "It's been empty since old man Cutter died, and it was pretty run-down before that."

"Besides, it's haunted." Chelsea shivered at the prospect. "Who'd want to live there?"

"Actually," Alyson defended her new home, "I think it's quite charming. In an old, run-down sort of way." She took a final bite of her apple, then wrapped the core in her napkin. Sitting on her hands, she crossed the first two fingers of *both* hands. "It may be a little rough, but I've lived there three weeks and I haven't seen any signs of other-worldly residents, so I don't think it's haunted." The last thing she wanted to do at this point was announce to her new friends that she'd been seeing ghosts. "It just needs a little work. A little elbow grease and it'll be good as new."

"I hear the place used to be quite spectacular in its heyday," Mac joined in. Taking a huge bite of her own greasy, ketchup-dripping hamburger, she chewed loudly, swallowed, and then continued her story. "It was originally built in 1845 by the town's founder, Jedediah Cutter. It used to be filled to the brim with antique furniture and elaborate artwork. Quite the showplace. Do you think any of that stuff could be up in the attic?"

"I have no idea," Alyson responded. "I guess we'll find out this weekend."

"I'm game for helping out with the cleaning." Mac's face lit up. "I'd love to get a peek at the inside of the place. I've always been sort of curious. Besides, who knows what goodies you might uncover? It'll be like a treasure hunt."

"Sure, the more the merrier."

"I'm in too," Trevor added. "I have football practice in the morning, but I could be there about noon. I was planning on going surfing with some of the guys from the team, but getting a look inside that old house is an opportunity I can't pass up."

"Well, I for one do not plan to spend my weekend wallowing around in a dusty attic." Chelsea stood up from the table and gathered her books. "Anyway, I'm going to Portland to shop for a new dress for the dance. But I'm totally up for the Cannery on Friday night. I hear Obsession is playing."

"Wow, they're really good," Mac agreed. "I heard their lead guitar player is in rehab, so they recruited some new guy from LA. He's supposed to be quite the babe."

"I wouldn't get too excited. From what *I* hear, this guy's just slightly more than totally out of your league." Chelsea put her foot on the chair she'd just vacated and smoothed the roll of her already perfectly rolled socks. She repeated the action with her other foot, then reached into her backpack for a mirror and lipstick.

"I didn't say I wanted to wrap him up and take him home," Mac shot back, "I just wanted to check him out. Besides, I'm not the one who's famous for shopping out of her league." Mac glanced toward Trevor.

"Well, I'll have you know—" Chelsea began

"So," Alyson interrupted, "how'd the house get so run-down anyway?"

"Barkley Cutter was a real recluse," Trevor answered, grateful for the timely interruption. "Story is, he never left the house for any reason. Someone in town delivered groceries and necessities to him once a week, and he never ventured out on his own."

"There are rumors of people in boats seeing someone walking along the cliffs near the house at night. Most people think it was him." Mac wadded up her greasy hamburger wrapper and tossed it toward the trash can, making a perfect basket.

"Pretty much would have to be because the old guy was a total kook who'd shoot at anyone who dared venture onto his property." Chelsea closed her compact and smoothed her hair.

"What happened to him?" Alyson asked. "He must have experienced some type of tragedy to turn him into such a loner."

"Story is," Trevor began, "his father, Jacob Cutter, was married to some rich society woman from San Francisco. She was never able to have children, but old Jacob had an illegitimate son by a bar maid in town. I guess he figured this child was the only one he was likely to have because his wife couldn't conceive, so he paid the woman a bunch of money and brought the son home to raise himself."

"I'm sure his wife was thrilled with that arrangement," Chelsea muttered under her breath as she picked up her books and walked away.

"I've heard she was abusive to the boy," Trevor continued. "To make matters worse, Jacob died when Barkley was only ten. He left his entire estate to him. The one stipulation was that his wife was to act as the boy's legal guardian until he reached the age of eighteen, and she was allowed to live in the house as long as she wanted.

"After that," Trevor elaborated, "the abuse got worse and worse. Most people think the lady lost her mind completely at some point. Anyway, on the night of Barkley's eighteenth birthday she fell to her death from the third-floor balcony."

"How awful." Alyson gasped. "Do you think Barkley killed her?"

"People around here think he pushed her, but it was never proven," Trevor answered. "Whatever happened that night must have been intense, though, because it was the last time anyone ever saw Barkley

Cutter. He holed himself up in that great big house of his and never came out again."

"How odd," Alyson marveled.

"Some people think whatever happened that night left Barkley badly scarred or deformed," Mac explained, "but no one really knows for sure."

"The delivery people from town must have seen him," Alyson retorted.

"No, they didn't." Mac leaned forward. "Every week someone would take supplies out to him and leave them on the porch. There would be an envelope with payment for the previous week's supplies and a list of what was to be delivered the next week."

"That's how they realized he was dead," Trevor explained. "When the delivery people went out to his place the previous week's supplies hadn't been picked up, so they went to get the sheriff."

"He was found dead in his bed." Mac shuddered. "He'd been dead for over a week."

"That's so sad," Alyson sympathized. "To live your whole life without any human contact whatsoever."

"There was a rumor," Mac whispered, as if sharing some deep, dark secret, "that Barkley did form a relationship with one of the delivery women, and the relationship resulted in the birth of a child. But it might just be a story."

"If there was a child there might be an heir," Alyson realized. "Has anyone tried to confirm the story? There should be hospital records, and probably a birth certificate. At the very least someone in town must have known the woman."

"As far as I know, no one's really done much to look for a possible heir," Trevor responded. "There were the usual announcements in the paper, but otherwise I doubt it."

"I wonder how hard it would be to do a little digging on our own," Alyson mused. "It doesn't seem right there might be a legal heir out there, but no one really tried to find him or her. Besides, what happens to the inheritance if no one comes forward? I mean, we paid money to a trust when we bought the house. Who gets that?"

"Good question," Mac agreed. "It'd be easy to do a little surfing on the Web. If there are any records I could probably find something."

"There are probably townsfolk around who still remember how the rumor got started in the first place," Trevor ventured. "Maybe someone remembers something specific that would at least give us a jumping-off point."

"If Barkley's stuff is still there, maybe there's a clue somewhere in the house itself," Mac contributed. "Have you gone through any of the desks or drawers?"

"Not really. We basically decided to make two of the bedrooms, a bathroom, and the kitchen habitable before tackling the rest of the house. The kitchen was a mess. We completely gutted it. There really wasn't much in there except some old pans and dishes and stuff. Nothing of value." Alyson noticed the time and began to gather up her stuff. "The two bedrooms each held a few pieces of furniture but no personal belongings. It looks like Barkley was using the bedroom off the kitchen, which might have originally been a maid's quarters, as his own. There's a bunch of stuff in there, but other than picking the junk off the floor and stripping the bed, we haven't gone through anything yet. It's a real mess. If there are any treasures or secrets hidden in the house they're bound to be in one of the other rooms. I can try to start looking around tonight. Let's talk more tomorrow."

Suddenly Alyson knew exactly what Barkley was trying to show her.

Chapter 4

The next morning Alyson opted for a black-and-navy-plaid wool miniskirt, a black fitted sweater, and knee-high boots. With the exception of the boots, the outfit reminded her of the plaid wool uniform she'd worn at the private high school she'd attended the year before. Who would have thought she'd actually miss that uniform? All of the girls at her school had hated it and spent a lot of time and money trying to personalize their look within the school's dress code. As Alyson looked at her reflection in the full-length mirror, she felt a sense of nostalgia. Somehow this outfit felt comforting, like an old familiar friend. She topped off her outfit with her black leather crop jacket and tried to remember the girl she had once been. The girl who just a few short months ago, along with her best friend Tiffany, had ruled Ms. James High School for Girls. Even though only five months had passed, it felt like a lifetime.

During those endless days immediately following the murder, Alyson could feel Tiff's presence as she told and retold her story and looked at mug shot after mug shot in an effort to bring her killers to justice. She could close her eyes and see Tiffany's auburn hair, smattering of freckles, and green eyes, which took on a mischievous glimmer as she threw caution to the winds and embraced life to its fullest, despite her stodgy upper-class pedigree. Now when she closed her eyes Alyson was greeted with silence. Tiffany was fading away. The more real Alyson became, the more Amanda and everything about her life faded into the darkness.

"What do you think of all the homework that was assigned for the second half of this week?" Alyson asked Mac as they walked toward the cafeteria after fourth period.

"It does seem like all the teachers got together and decide to send us into homework overload," Mac complained. "Do you want to get together after school and work on our English project?"

"I have to meet my mom right after school, but I can catch up with you around three thirty." Alyson was hesitant to mention her previously scheduled DMV appointment. She was sure most if not all of her new friends had gotten their licenses months ago. She'd seen Mac driving an old, beat-up Volkswagen Bug, and Trevor had an awesome Mustang that looked to be either a '65 or '66.

"That'd be fine. I'll meet you in the school library. It should be open until five o'clock or so."

"Sounds like a plan."

The Seacliff High library was quaint and cozy, not at all what Alyson expected. The books were shelved in mahogany bookcases that were arranged along all four walls on two levels. The first level shelves were about six feet tall with two sets of stairs, one on each end of the room, leading to the second level stacks. The ceiling was high, allowing for the two levels to be open to each other. In the center of the room on the bottom level was an array of dark hardwood tables surrounded with hardwood chairs.

The room was small but charming, much like the libraries she remembered from the European estates she'd visited in her old life. The elegance and beauty didn't quite fit with the run-down condition of the rest of the school. The bookshelves themselves must have cost a fortune.

"Good, no one's here," Mac said, walking up behind her as she continued to drink in the rich ambience of the room. "We shouldn't have to do the whole whispering thing."

"This place is great." Alyson walked over to one of the hardwood tables and set her backpack down. "I love libraries. Especially the way they smell, sort of musty and ancient. It's as if all the knowledge of the ages are contained within their walls. And this library in particular; it's so welcoming."

"Yeah, I love it in here," Mac agreed. "I often come in to study, and the place is usually deserted. It's nice and quiet, not like at home."

"Do you have brothers and sisters?"

"Yeah, a brother and two sisters. I love them to death, but they can really stir up a ruckus and make it hard to concentrate. How about you? Any siblings?"

"No, it's just me and my mom. Sometimes I think my house is way too quiet. A little ruckus might be nice for a change."

"Well, I'd be glad to lend you my sisters anytime. I'm sure they'd change your mind in no time."

"Yeah, maybe." Alyson sighed wistfully. "The library is a lot bigger than I thought it would be. Do you think there are any books on the Cutter family or the house?"

"Probably." Mac strolled over to the section of shelves that housed the local history books. She pulled several off the shelf and returned to the table.

"This book covers the town's origins. There might be something in here." Mac opened the book and started to read. "Oh, look. Here's a chapter on the Cutter family. 'Jedediah Cutter, the town's founder, was born in 1802 in Boston, Massachusetts. He was the eldest son of Brandon Cutter, a third-generation shipping magnate. In 1822 he migrated west and started his own shipping line, increasing his wealth a hundredfold. He established the town of Cutter's Cove in 1842.'"

"Does it say how much he was worth?" Alyson asked.

Mac skimmed the pages. "No, not really. A lot, I imagine. 'In 1826 he built the house on the bluff and married his childhood sweetheart, who bore him a son, Marcus, in 1828, and twin daughters, Estelle and Isabel, in 1830.'"

"The house is older than I thought. Can you imagine the history? The lives that have played out within its walls. If those walls could talk imagine the stories they could tell."

"Yeah, it's pretty awesome to consider. Maybe we'll find something personal in the attic—pictures, or better yet a diary of some long-ago resident."

"Maybe I'll check out a few of these books. It makes the house seem somehow more alive to know its history. I can almost imagine the faces of the people who walked the same halls I walk every day and slept in the same room I sleep in at night."

"Maybe the house really is haunted and you'll get to meet some of the previous residents. Just think of the questions you could ask, the secrets you could uncover."

"Yeah, it'd be pretty awesome. Now I guess we should get to our Chem homework," Alyson said. "Maybe we'll have time to tackle the calculus too."

The girls worked in companionable cooperation until the library closed at five and they each went home for dinner.

Chapter 5

The next couple of days flew by, and before she knew it, Alyson found herself once again standing in front of her full-length mirror, frowning at her reflection. If she were going to a club in New York she'd know exactly what to wear, but what did one wear to an abandoned fish cannery turned quasi nightclub in upstate Oregon? So far, all she'd managed was to pick out her favorite Italian lingerie and now stood wearing nothing else as she stared into the mirror. She twisted her long hair on top of her head, letting tendrils fall around her shoulders in a haphazard fashion. Her makeup was understated yet perfectly applied to accentuate every asset and minimize every flaw. Her experience as a model was serving her well.

She looked absolutely perfect, a natural beauty who didn't have to try too hard. A practically naked natural beauty, she reminded herself. She really did need to decide on a dress. Mac was going to be here to pick her up in a matter of minutes. She stared at the pile on the bed once again and finally settled on a simple soft blue shirtdress she'd found in a little shop in SoHo. Some thigh-high, boot-wearing go-go girl in the sixties probably wore the simple minidress originally. It fit her perfectly, accentuating her long legs and flat stomach. She opted for her new crop boots over her knee-high ones, giving the vintage dress a modern look. Grabbing her old standby leather crop jacket and handbag, she headed downstairs to wait for Mac.

The club was rustic, to say the least, but the energy from the dancing patrons and the exceptional quality of the band put the place on a par with any of New York's hot spots to Alyson's mind. The place had once been an actual fish cannery that had closed quite a few years earlier. Some budding entrepreneurs from San Francisco had bought the property and turned it into a nightclub/burger joint, complete with a shiny dance floor, a large octagon-shaped stage, and elaborate lighting and sound systems. Actually, as Alyson took a closer look at her surroundings, she realized any similarities to a New York club ended there. The bar served Budweiser instead of Cristal and burgers instead of sushi, and was lined with pool tables rather than VIP booths. The place was charming and totally unpretentious. Alyson loved it immediately.

"Do you want a soda?" Mac yelled over the noise of the band. "I thought we'd get drinks and look for Trevor. He said he'd meet us here."

"Sounds good," Alyson yelled back, following Mac to the bar. They ordered Diet Cokes, then looked for a table that would provide them with the best vantage point for checking out the band's newest member.

"Wow, this place is great." Alyson sat down at the table next to Mac. "Who would have thought a sleepy little town like Cutter's Cove would have a great club like this?"

"Yeah, it's pretty hot. People come all the way from Portland on Friday nights to hear the bands. Hey, there's Trevor," she said, waving toward the door. "Oh, great." Mac groaned. "Chelsea's with him."

"Yeah, and what's with the outfit?" Alyson asked. "She looks like she's dressed for the red carpet."

Chelsea wore a long red dress tight enough to leave little to the imagination. There was a slit all the way up one leg and the back was cut low enough to leave no question regarding the bra/no bra debate. In fact, between the slit up the leg and the extremely low back, it left no doubt as to the underwear/ no underwear question either.

"She looks like a hooker," Mac agreed. "She can't possibly have a stitch on underneath. I can't wait to see how she's going to sit down."

"Ladies," Trevor greeted as the pair approached the table and sat down next to Alyson. "Some band, huh? I bet you didn't have anything like this in Minnesota."

"No, I can't say we did," Alyson crossed her fingers and answered, having no idea whether there were clubs in Minnesota or not.

Chelsea leaned against the table, sort of half-sitting on it. "Trev, be a doll and get me something to drink. A Bellini, if they have it."

"Chelsea, you're sixteen, not twenty-one. How about a soda?"

"Sure, whatever."

"So, Chelsea, why don't you have a seat?" Mac prompted.

"No, thanks, I'm fine. I have a better view of that hunky new band member. He hasn't been able to take his eyes off me since we walked in the door."

"Yeah, I'm sure that dress caught everyone's attention." Mac smirked.

"It's quite fabulous, isn't it? I see Courtney and the others over by the bar. I think I'll wander over and show it off."

"Courtney?" Alyson asked as Chelsea walked away.

"She's one of the A-list crowd, along with Chelsea and the other cheerleaders. The only reason Chelsea lowers herself enough to be seen in our humble company is because of Trevor. He totally refuses to hang with them, so if she wants to hang with Trevor, she has to put up with us."

Alyson smiled. Some things never changed. Her old school had its social hierarchy too, at which she'd been smack dab on the top. Oh, how the mighty had fallen.

"Let's dance." Alyson grabbed Mac's hand and led her toward the dance floor. The pair merged into the crowd, forgetting all about Chelsea, her ridiculous dress, and her snobbery.

Chapter 6

The next morning Mac showed up bright and early, despite the lateness of the previous night's partying.

"How about some coffee?" a slightly less energetic Alyson offered.

"No, thanks. I never drink coffee; it makes me jumpy."

Alyson poured her third cup of the morning and sat down at the kitchen table. "After hearing the story about this house, I've really been excited about checking out the stuff upstairs. Maybe there's some old and valuable stuff left from generations of Cutters. I'd love to find out more about the previous occupants of the house. Who they were, how they lived, what it might have been like to live here all those years ago."

"Well, let's get started then." Mac jumped up in her usual energetic manner and headed toward the stairs leading to the attic.

"Okay." Alyson groaned, refilling her coffee cup again and bringing it with her. "We'll stop off upstairs so I can introduce you to my mom. She's really great."

The pair climbed the stairs to the second floor, stepping over drop cloths and cans of paint.

"Mom, this is my friend Mac." Alyson gestured toward her as they made their way into the room.

"Mac, Mom." She nodded toward the slim woman perched precariously on a tall, rickety ladder.

"I'm happy to meet you. Alyson has told me so much about you."

"It's great to meet you too." Mac looked around the room. "I love the wallpaper."

"Alyson picked it out. I really like the way it's turning out. Are you girls headed up to the attic?"

"Yeah. I just wanted to stop off on our way up to introduce you and see how the room was coming along."

"There's a lot of stuff up there." Alyson's mom turned slightly so she was half-sitting on the top rung of the ladder. "Don't hurt yourself carrying those heavy boxes down the stairs."

"Trevor is coming by this afternoon to help out too. We'll save the heavy stuff for his manly muscles," Alyson assured her mom as she headed out the door and started up the stairs toward the attic

"Oh my gosh," Mac gushed from behind her on the stairs. "Your mom looks exactly like you. Or maybe you look like her?" she corrected. "At any rate, you look exactly alike. You could practically be twins."

"People think we're sisters all the time," Alyson confirmed. "She looks really young for her age and has this sort of quirky, youthful air about her." Or at least, Alyson thought to herself, she did before the murder. Now she seemed serious and worried a lot of the time.

"It'd be so cool to have a young, hip mom. My mom's a lot more, you know, momish. Short hair, sensible shoes, polyester pants; she definitely has that whole middle-aged mom look about her. Don't get me wrong; she's a great mom—most of the time, anyway. But there's no way anyone would mistake us for sisters. At least I hope not. Wow." Mac stared in wonder after completing the four-story climb to the top of the house. "You weren't kidding about the amount of stuff stored up here."

"I know." Alyson stood next to her, wondering where to start. "I can't even see much past the first couple of rows of boxes, and the room looks like it's probably pretty big if it mirrors the size of the other three floors."

"I guess we'd better get started." Mac opened the first box. "Oh my God," she shrieked as she jumped back through the doorway.

"What's the matter?" Alyson ran to her friend's side.

"There's something in that box. Something dead."

"Oh, God, it isn't, is it?"

"No, not a person. A rabbit, I think, or maybe a raccoon. It just startled me. I opened the box expecting to find old dishes or discarded paperwork, not the skeleton of some long-dead animal."

Alyson walked over and lifted the lid of the box. "I see what you mean. Maybe we should wait for Trevor before sorting through this particular box. I'll just move it off to the side."

Mac gingerly opened the next box and began sorting its contents. "It may be the dead rodent talking, but doesn't this place seem a little creepy? It feels like someone's watching me."

"Do you believe in ghosts?"

Mac stopped working. "Yeah, I guess. Why do you ask? Do you see one?"

"Not now, but I did. At least I think I did. I didn't tell you before because I didn't want you to think I was psycho before you got a chance to know me."

"Who was it?"

"Barkley Cutter, I think. One night I woke up and saw him standing at the foot of my bed. The door to the attic had been rusted shut since we moved in, but I followed him up the stairs and the door just opened with no effort at all."

"Wow. I think I'd die of a heart attack if I saw a ghost at the foot of my bed. Were you scared?"

"Sort of, but not really. Like you said about feeling like someone was watching you, I'd felt him watching me for days. When I woke up and saw him it was like I'd been expecting him. I think he wants us to find something. I think he left behind a secret when he died. Maybe it has to do with a possible heir, maybe it's something else, but I'm pretty sure the answer is up here."

"Now I'm really anxious to sort through this stuff, but Barkley, if you're listening, no late-night visits to my bedroom, please. I'm afraid I'm not as brave as Alyson."

Four hours later, Alyson pushed her hands into the small of her back to ease the soreness that was starting to develop there. "I'm starved. How about taking a break for some lunch?"

"We've been working all morning and we haven't even made a dent." Mac groaned.

"Maybe things will go faster once Trevor shows up. Where is he anyway? It's almost twelve thirty; didn't he say he'd be here by noon?"

"That's Trevor for you." Mac set the box she'd been looking through to the side. "He's usually late. But he'll be here. He was as excited about going through this stuff as I was, but that was before I found out about the ghost. I hope we can discover what Barkley wants you to find."

"So far all we've found is a bunch of old clothes, broken appliances, and boxes of paperwork," Alyson complained.

"It makes sense that if there's anything valuable up here it would be toward the back. Everything we've come across so far was probably put here by Barkley during his later years. Besides," Mac reached her hands over her head and leaned from side to side, "we might find some clues to his missing heir in these boxes of paperwork once we get a chance to go through them."

Alyson started toward the stairs. "You're right. Let's go down and make some lunch before I completely fade away."

"Lunch sounds good."

In the kitchen, Alyson opened the refrigerator and began rummaging around for ingredients to make sandwiches. Her mom hadn't really done much in the way of grocery shopping since they'd moved into the house. First there hadn't been a functioning kitchen, and then they'd been so busy with the remodel it seemed easiest to make sandwiches or go out to eat.

"I think I hear Trevor now," Alyson said, walking to open the door leading off the kitchen and out to the yard. "Who's the guy with him?"

"I have no idea." Mac stared at the exceptionally tall and exceptionally handsome blond god who was getting out of Trevor's car.

"Hey, guys," Trevor said as he approached the back porch. "This is Eli Stevenson. He just moved here from California. Eli, meet Alyson and Mac."

"Come on in." Alyson stepped aside to let them in. "We were just going to have some lunch. You guys hungry?"

"Starved," they responded in unison

"Eli's the new receiver on the football team," Trevor explained as they settled into the chairs surrounding the kitchen table. "I hope it's okay that I brought him along."

"It's great," Mac blurted out a little too enthusiastically. "I mean, there's a huge mess upstairs and we could really use an extra pair of hands."

"How about ham sandwiches and leftover potato salad?" Alyson asked. "The ham's from dinner last night and I can vouch for its yummy goodness."

"Sounds good," the others agreed.

"So, Eli," Mac focused her attention on the new addition to the group, "why did your family move all the way up here from California?"

"My dad owns his own company. He specializes in customized software for select clients. He can work from anywhere, and he was sick of the noise and pollution in SoCal, so we packed up and moved here after my mom died."

"What type of software does he write?" Mac asked.

"All kinds, really. Right now he's working on some type of security software for a large company back east, but he's done games and business applications too."

"Wow, I'd love to see some of the stuff he's developed."

"Sure, any time."

"Mac's our computer genius," Trevor explained. "She probably thinks she just fell into computer heaven."

"I'm just interested," Mac defended herself, looking away.

"I'm sure my dad would be happy to talk to you. He loves to talk about his work, and frankly, except for the games, I'm not all that interested."

During lunch the girls filled the guys in on their progress, Alyson told them about her visit from Barkley, and everyone filled Eli in on the history of the house. By the time they'd had their fill of the delicious lunch, they were charged up to resume the adventure in the attic.

"The stuff that's obviously junk, like the small appliances and broken knickknacks, we're bagging up and taking to the trash pile in the yard," Alyson explained as they resumed work. "Anything that has no value to us but might to someone else, like clothes in decent condition or undamaged bric-a-brac, we're putting in the room nearest to the front door. There's a bunch of old furniture in there, but we've pushed it back and started a pile right inside the door. If you find boxes with paperwork or anything that might be of interest, we're putting it in the empty room to the right of the stairs on the floor below this one."

"You weren't kidding about the volume of stuff up here." Trevor sounded awed. "It'll take weeks to get through all this stuff. I saw a bunch of things in the back of the room covered with old sheets. Maybe that's the valuable stuff."

"That's the advantage of height," Mac declared. "Alyson and I couldn't see any farther into the room than the first couple of rows. What do you think might be under the sheets?"

"I have no idea." Trevor stood on his tiptoes to try to get a better look. "I really can't make out any shapes. I guess we'd better get working so we can get back there to find out."

The next few hours provided nothing of much interest except a few more boxes of papers to go through later. Well into the third hour of work, however, Eli alerted the others to a possible find.

"Hey, guys, check this out," he said, holding up a small painting.

"Oh my God, it looks like a Monet," Mac exclaimed.

"I'm sure it's just a copy," Trevor speculated. "Who would keep a genuine Monet in the attic?"

"No, it looks real," Alyson confirmed, taking a closer look at the object in question.

"How can you tell?" Mac asked.

"I used to have . . ." She paused and crossed her fingers behind her back, "a friend," she stuttered, "who had one. Of course, we'd have to take it to an art dealer to have it authenticated, but my guess is it's the real thing."

"This painting must be worth thousands," Trevor predicted.

"At least," Alyson confirmed.

"I can't wait to get to the stuff under the sheets. This painting wasn't even covered," Eli added.

"So is this stuff all yours?" Mac asked. "I mean, you bought the house with the stuff in it, so it seems whatever you find must belong to you, right?"

"I guess. But I'd still like to find Barkley's child if he or she exists. Somehow it doesn't seem right to keep someone else's legacy."

"Yeah, I guess you're right." Mac carried the box of old dishes she had been looking through to the door and set it aside to be carried downstairs by one of the boys later. "But can you imagine what it would be like to have hundreds of thousands, maybe even millions of dollars?"

"Actually," Alyson ventured, "I'll bet it wouldn't be any better than this. Good friends, a quiet and safe place to live, an unfolding mystery to try to solve. And we can't forget about the kick-ass football team that's sure to take state."

"You said it," Trevor and Eli shouted, giving each other a high-five.

"Are you going to the dance next Saturday?" Mac asked Eli. "Because if you are, you can go with us. We're all going together."

Alyson smiled when she noticed the coy way in which Mac was looking at Eli. *You go girl*, she thought to herself.

"Sure; it sounds like fun," Eli answered.

Alyson looked out the window to see the sun setting over the ocean beyond. "Maybe we should call it quits for the day. It's getting late and I'm beat."

"Yeah, I should go," Mac agreed. "Mom will want me home for dinner."

"Thank you, guys, for all your hard work. I can't believe we're only halfway through the room," Alyson said.

"I can come back tomorrow if you want," Mac offered.

"That'd be great."

"I'm in too," Trevor added.

"Me too," Eli piped in. "This has actually been really fun, and after finding the painting I'm curious about what else we might find."

"We probably shouldn't mention the painting to anyone at this point," Trevor suggested. "If people found out there might be valuable objects in the house it could provide a security risk, and with Alyson and her mom out here in the middle of nowhere with no one else around . . ."

"You've got a good point," Mac agreed. "For now, let's just keep the whole project to ourselves. And maybe we shouldn't mention old Barkley's visit to Alyson either. The idea of a real ghost is bound to attract a lot of attention."

"So how'd your day go?" Mom inquired from behind her as the group drove away. "Did you get the room cleared out?"

"Not even close." Alyson moaned as she leaned back into her mom for support.

Alyson's mom wrapped her arms around her from behind.

"I'd say we're halfway through," Alyson continued.

"I'm about halfway through with the painting and wallpapering in the two bedrooms. They look really nice, though. Want to see?'

"Sure," Alyson said, standing up straight. "I love the colors I picked out. I can't wait to see how everything turns out. I think I'll get matching curtains, and maybe a new duvet."

"I think you'll be pleased," her mom answered, leading her by the hand up the stairs. "The furniture we ordered should be here any day."

"Oh, Mom, it's great!" Alyson exclaimed, walking into the freshly painted room. "I thought you said you were only half-done, though. Looks done to me."

"I am only half-done. I just did your half first."

"You're the best mom ever." Alyson hugged her mom tight. "I love the way the blue in the wallpaper blends with the light gray paint. I saw some curtains in Portland the other day that would match perfectly. Maybe I'll get some contrasting throw pillows for the bed. You know; blue, gray, blue, gray."

"I get it." Her mom laughed. "I'm glad you like the room. I want you to feel comfortable and at home in this house."

"I'm feeling snuggly already. Let's go look at your room, and then I have something to show you upstairs. I think you'll be surprised."

"That's a Monet," her mom trilled a few minutes later, after Alyson had led her upstairs to see the painting. "You found this in the attic?"

"Yup, buried under a pile of junk."

"Who would store a painting of this value underneath a pile of junk?"

"It's obvious Barkley wasn't all that stable, and who knows about the generations preceding him?" Alyson turned off the light in the room where they were storing the more valuable finds and started down the stairs, "The gang and I are going to do some research on the family and its history to try to find out if the rumor about Barkley having a child is true. If there is an heir it'd be nice to find him or her."

"Well, good luck with the digging, but be careful. Your insatiable curiosity has gotten you into quite a lot of trouble in the past."

"I know, Mom." Alyson squeezed her hand. "Don't worry. I'll be careful. I promise. Mom? Do you believe in ghosts?"

Chapter 7

As promised, the gang showed up bright and early the next morning. "Muffins, anyone?" Alyson asked as they filed in through the kitchen door. "Blueberry. Homemade from a box."

"I'll take one," Trevor said, grabbing two.

Alyson set the plate of muffins beside the pitcher of orange juice on the kitchen table.

"Did you get a chance to go through any of the papers last night?" Mac asked, sitting down at the table and pouring herself a glass of the fresh-squeezed juice.

"No. I took the three most promising-looking boxes down to my room, but then my mom suggested we go into town for dinner, and by the time we got back I was so tired I just went to bed."

"After Eli found the painting yesterday, I was so jazzed to continue the hunt for buried treasure I could barely sleep at all." Mac picked at her muffin.

"Yeah," Trevor agreed. "I just know today we're going to find a lot more interesting things than we did yesterday."

"Well, let's get to it, then." Alyson picked up a muffin for the road and headed toward the stairs leading to the attic.

"I can't wait to see what's under those sheets." Alyson turned her head to speak to the party behind her as she made the long climb up the four flights.

"At the very least there should be some old furniture, and maybe some family pic . . ." She stopped dead at the top of the stairs, letting her last sentence dangle.

"What the . . ."

"Oh my God," Mac screeched from beside her. "What happened?"

"Did you come back up here last night after we left?" Trevor asked.

When they'd left the attic the previous night the things that hadn't yet been sorted had been stacked in the back of the room. Now, everything had been moved to the sides, with a path carved out in the center. Some of the furniture that had still been covered with sheets the previous evening was now bare. It was obvious someone had been in there.

"No." Alyson stepped a little farther into the room and stared in shocked silence.

"Maybe your mom?" Trevor suggested.

"No, she was as exhausted as I was and went straight to bed when we got home."

"Did you hear anything strange last night?" Trevor questioned. "Like someone moving around up here?"

"No. Like I said, I was really exhausted, but I didn't hear anything."

"Maybe you should go ask your mom if she did," Trevor advised.

"Can't." Alyson walked farther into the room, continuing to stare at the sight that had greeted them. "She went into Portland to order some stuff for the bedrooms she's remodeling."

"Okay, if you didn't come up here last night and we assume your mom didn't either, who did?" Trevor wondered.

"It's obvious someone moved everything all around." Eli examined a large trunk sitting toward the front of the room that hadn't been there the day before.

"I think there are really only three possibilities," Mac commented. "Either Alyson's mom did come up here at some point," Mac held up one finger, "or someone broke in at some point and moved everything around." Finger number two was raised. "Or Barkley either didn't like us moving his stuff around yesterday or he wanted us to hurry up and find the trunk." A third finger completed the countdown. "All of this furniture was buried in the back of the room," she added, walking farther into the room. "It must have taken someone hours to move all this stuff."

"Even if Alyson's mom did come up here, I doubt she moved this trunk. It probably weighs several hundred pounds." Eli tried to give the trunk a shove and it barely moved. "And although the ghost idea sounds kind of cool, I don't think ghosts can move things. That leaves the break-in theory."

"This is too weird." Alyson shuddered, moving closer for a better look at the trunk.

"Has any of the stuff we moved into the room downstairs been disturbed?" Mac asked, peeking around the corner of the very old-looking bureau she'd been examining.

"I don't know. Let's check," Alyson said, standing up from her squatting position in front of the chest.

The third to the top stair squeaked loudly four times as each of them traveled over it to the floor below. "You'd think you would have heard that if someone went up the stairs after you went to bed," Mac observed.

"I doubt it. I was pretty tired."

No one said anything as they stared into the room on the third floor. The contents of all of the boxes had been strewn around the floor.

"I'd say someone was looking for something," Eli observed.

"Yeah, but who? And when?" Alyson wondered.

"Maybe while you were in town for dinner," Trevor ventured. "Or maybe after you went to bed."

Alyson shuddered again at the thought that someone might have been in the house while she slept in the bedroom below.

Mac picked up a pile of the tossed papers. "I wonder what they were looking for. And even more important, I wonder if they found it?"

"There's really no way to tell if anything was taken," Eli added.

"They left the painting," Mac noted. "Whoever did this was obviously after something specific. A random thief would have taken the painting for sure."

"Unless they didn't know anything about art and didn't realize the painting's possible value," Alyson postulated. "Let's look around upstairs to see what we find. We won't know if anything's missing because we have no idea what was up there, but at least we can see if whoever broke in left anything of value behind. What he didn't take might give us a clue as to what he was after."

They headed back upstairs and spent the next several hours sifting through the remainder of the attic's contents. They uncovered several boxes of children's toys that appeared to be quite old; a variety of dishes and other kitchen items of varying age and state of repair; clothing that looked like it might have dated back to the turn of the century or even earlier; additional artwork; and quite a few pieces of old furniture Alyson was sure would produce a tidy sum on the antiques market. And of course there was the trunk, which they managed to shove over to the wall by the door. It appeared to be fairly old, and the workmanship was quite fine, so they decided to do a thorough search of the house to see if they could find the key before resorting to destroying the lock.

With everything sorted and moved into the room below except for the trunk, which was too heavy to move, they headed downstairs for a well-deserved lunch break.

Alyson created a sort of make-your-own-sandwich bar on the counter from the hodge-podge of ingredients available in the refrigerator, and the hungry teens helped themselves to heaping plates of food, then gathered around the table to eat.

"Maybe you should call the police," Trevor said after taking several large bites of his ham sandwich.

"No!" Alyson barked. "I mean, I don't really think that's necessary," she added in a more controlled voice.

"It does look like someone may have broken in here sometime last night," Mac said persuasively.

"Possibly, but we don't know for sure, and it looks like the intruder was looking for something pretty specific because there were tons of really valuable things left totally undisturbed. Maybe he found what he was looking for and that's the end of it."

"Yeah, but what if he comes back? It's only you and your mom out here all alone," Mac argued. "You don't even have any neighbors within shouting distance."

"I appreciate your concern, but we'll be fine. Really." All Alyson needed at this point was to draw attention to herself with the local authorities. Not very stealthy. Her mom was going to totally freak when she heard what had happened.

"I really think we're better off keeping this between us for now. If we go to the cops the story will end up in the newspaper, and then the whole town will know there's a bunch of valuable stuff out here. We might end up with more potential prowlers than if we just keep quiet."

"Yeah, I guess," Mac agreed tentatively, still doubtful.

"At least let me shore up your nonexistent security," Trevor insisted. "A two year old could pick the lock on the kitchen door and the lock on the window over the sink is totally broken. Anyone could walk in here at any time with little trouble and no warning."

"You might have a point there." Alyson nodded.

"Eli and I will go into town after lunch and get some supplies, then come back out and secure this place the best we can before we leave tonight."

"You should get a dog," Mac advised. "A really big dog. At least no one could sneak up on you."

A dog. Alyson considered the idea. She'd always wanted a dog, but before this she'd lived in an apartment. A dog would be fun. "I'll ask my mom," she said, warming up to the idea.

After lunch the boys went into town for supplies and the girls stayed behind to clean up.

"So what are you planning to wear to the dance on Saturday night?" Alyson asked Mac as they worked together to wash the lunch dishes. "You said it was casual, but what exactly does that mean?"

"Anything goes really," Mac answered. "Jeans, cords, skirts, sweaters, tanks. The only requirement is that you wear some combination of the school colors."

"Which are?"

"Royal blue and gray."

"Sounds doable."

"Sometimes people dress up like the school mascot, which is a pirate, but I guarantee Chelsea will be the only one there in formal wear, if she does indeed go that route."

"She really goes overboard in the trying-to-impress department."

"You can say that again. It's all about her hair, her figure, her clothes, and of course her popularity. If everyone doesn't totally adore her at all times or anyone does anything that might interfere in any way with said adoration, she totally goes into hysterics." Mac wiped the counter free of crumbs. "During cheerleading tryouts last year this poor girl, who truly had no coordination whatsoever, accidentally tripped Chelsea during the group routine, causing her to fall on her perky little behind. Chelsea went ballistic, threatening the girl with all kinds of nasty outcomes if her little blunder in any way kept her from making the team. Luckily, Chelsea made the team anyway, and as far as I know the girl dropped out of the competition and faded into the woodwork, like the rest of us mere mortals."

"She must be really insecure to feel she has to try so hard," Alyson observed.

"Maybe." Mac considered that possibility. "Up to this point I just figured she was born with an extra dose of the bitch gene, but you might have a point. I mean, it must be exhausting to be her. All that waxing, bleaching, tanning, and buffing she does. Not to mention the hours she spends painting on that face every morning. And Samantha Jones told me she takes a spinning class every morning before school."

"Wow." Alyson was impressed at her commitment. "Who knew beauty could take so much work?"

"You're quite the looker yourself," Mac observed, "and I don't see you doing all that."

"Thanks for the compliment, but I'm not in the same league as Chelsea."

"You're kidding, right? You don't have to go all modest with me. Every girl in the whole school pretty much hated you on sight, with your perfect silky blond hair, long legs, and absence of even the slightest trace of fat cells."

"Every girl in the whole school hates me?"

"Don't worry. I was just making a point." Mac laughed. "Most of the girls don't even know you, and those who do adore you. Well, except possibly for Chelsea. But she's just jealous. You must realize that without even trying, you pose a big threat in the boyfriend market."

"Thanks; I adore you too," Alyson echoed, deciding to steer the conversation away from her looks and on to something more interesting, like friendship. "I can't tell you how much I value the friendship I've developed with you and Trevor and Eli. I was a little worried coming to a new school that's so vastly different from anything I'm used to, that I wouldn't fit in."

"Seacliff High can't be that much different from high schools in Minnesota. It's not like you're from Los Angeles or New York or something,"

"True." Alyson quickly crossed her fingers. "It's just that any time you do something new, it's different."

"I guess," Mac agreed. "I heard a car pull up out front. Maybe it's the boys."

"We're back," Eli greeted them, coming in first through the kitchen door.

"Let's get to work," Trevor said. "We have a lot of ground to cover and not much time."

"I'll start at the front of the house," Eli volunteered.

The group worked amicably for the reminder of the afternoon, and by the time everyone left at around six o'clock the house was locked up tighter than Fort Knox.

Of course Alyson would have to explain the reason for the increased security to her mom when she returned from Portland, and while she was less than thrilled and more than a little concerned, to say the least, she agreed it was best to keep things quiet, and a very large, very loud dog was a most excellent idea.

That night Alyson sorted through the first three boxes of papers in her room. There were a lot of old receipts, newspaper clippings, and bank records. Most of the information seemed insignificant, but she took a closer look at the bank statements, spreading them out on her bed. "Okay, Barkley. What am I looking for?"

A gust of wind from the open window scattered the paperwork, causing one of the bank statements to fall to the floor. Alyson bent to pick it up and took a closer look. "Wait a minute. What do we have here?"

Chapter 8

On Monday morning Alyson couldn't wait to tell her friends about her findings, but Chelsea was within listening distance during first period, and it wouldn't really be fair to Eli, who didn't share any classes with Alyson, Trevor, or Mac, to discuss the situation in his absence.

"So," Alyson blurted out as soon as she sat down at their regular lunch table near the window, "you'll never guess what I found in those boxes of papers last night."

"Spill," Trevor encouraged, as anxious to hear what she had to say as she was to say it.

"One of the boxes contained a bunch of financial receipts, which, judging by the dates, must have belonged to Barkley. I came across a check register showing a ten-thousand-dollar deposit into an account through Cutter's Cove Community Bank. There were a number of expenditures, including monthly utility bills, a weekly check to the Cutter's Cove Market, and various checks to other local stores here and there. The really interesting thing, though," Alyson took a bite of her sandwich, pausing for dramatic effect, "is that every month between September 1955 and May 1968 there was a check made out to Mary Swanson."

"You think she was the mother of his illegitimate child?" Mac dipped the end of her corn dog in the mustard on her plate.

"I'm not sure," Alyson admitted. "I just found it interesting that Barkley would be paying this woman a good chunk of change every month for thirteen years."

"Yeah, but why only thirteen years?" Trevor queried after doing the math. "If old Barkley was paying some type of child support don't you think he would have done so until the child turned at least eighteen?"

"Maybe," Alyson said. "The reality is, she could have been a cleaning lady or some other type of regular help. But it's a start. I think it would be worth our while to research Mary a little more thoroughly."

"I agree." Mac started making a few notes on a yellow legal pad. "I could search local hospital and county records online to see if there's any documentation of a birth related to Mary. I could also find out if there are any records indicating where we might find her at this point in time." Mac continued to scribble notes as she spoke. "I'd also be interested in where the money that was deposited in Barkley's account each month came from." She stopped writing and bit the end of her pen. "That may be a little harder to backtrack. Banks tend to have pretty good security systems, so hacking in might take a while."

"My dad's out of town. You could come over to my place to do your search if you want," Eli offered. "We probably have some software you wouldn't otherwise have access to."

"That'd be great." Mac started writing furiously again. "Is after school okay?"

"I get done with football practice around four thirty. Meet me by the door to the boys' gym and we'll go to my house from there."

"If Mac and Eli are going to work on the computer record, I think I'll go into town to try to talk to some of the town's senior residents. Someone must still be around who would remember Mary. Want to come with me, Trevor? I could use a local along who knows the town and its people. To be honest, I'd have no idea where to start otherwise."

"Sure, why not? I'll meet you at the gym after practice."

The rest of the day flew by as Alyson waited impatiently for four thirty to roll around. She'd already called her mom to tell her she'd be eating dinner in town with her friends. She had a real feeling about this Mary. It wasn't like she was psychic or anything, but she often got a sort of tingly feeling deep in her gut when things were about to be blown wide open. Besides, Barkley seemed to want her to find the specific records pertaining to Mary. It hadn't been windy at all the night before. Not even a breeze. The sudden gust of wind had to have come from Barkley's spirit.

After computer lab Alyson went to the library to get a start on her homework. She arrived at the boys' gym promptly at 4:15 and found Mac leaning against the wall waiting.

"Been here long?" Alyson asked.

"Just a few minutes. I decided to do my homework before coming over."

"Me too. I just came from the library. I hope the guys don't fall behind. We're keeping them pretty busy. And with football and all . . ."

"Trevor's really smart, and he's only taking two AP classes. I think he'll be fine. And even though we don't know Eli all that well, he seems pretty capable."

"Yeah, I guess." Alyson leaned against the wall next to Mac. "As long as we have this figured out by midterms at least."

"We will," Mac promised. "I have this feeling deep in my gut that things are about to start falling into place."

"I was just thinking the same thing. It's like I feel we're on the verge of some great epiphany."

"People are starting to come out," Mac observed. "We'll talk some more tomorrow at lunch."

"Actually," Alyson said, searching the emerging crowd for Trevor and Eli, "I'm sort of surprised Chelsea didn't join us at lunch today. I was afraid she would. She sat with us every day last week."

"I heard the cheerleaders are holding extra practices at lunch all this week in preparation for Friday's game and Saturday's parade. I think we'll be okay this week. But next week, who knows?"

By the time she finished speaking the boys had joined them, and each pair walked off its separate ways.

"So where do we start?" Trevor asked once they were seated in his 1965 Mustang convertible.

"I'm not really sure. I figure if Mary had been Barkley's secret mistress, she would have to be at least in her seventies if she's still around. We need to talk to people who would have been alive during the time of her supposed pregnancy, so we're talking the more senior of the town's residents."

"There's a retired schoolteacher who still lives in town. My dad told me he had her in the fourth grade, so she must have been teaching during the sixties. Actually, if Mary did have a child, and he or she did go to school here, he or she would probably have gone to elementary school the same time my dad did."

"I guess you could ask your dad if he remembers anyone with the last name of Swanson. Although it might seem weird because we don't know if we're talking about a boy or a girl."

"Yeah, but that gives me an idea. We should have Mac search school records for a student with the last name of Swanson. He or she would have been in elementary school from . . ." Trevor mentally did the math, "approximately 1960 to 1966, give or take a year."

"I'll try to reach her on her cell," Alyson offered, pulling her own cell phone from her purse.

"Tell her to check junior high and high school records while she's at it," Trevor added after they connected.

"Okay, now what?" Alyson asked, clicking off her phone and sliding it back into her purse.

"If our theory is correct Mary would have been working as a delivery person for Cutter's Cove Market at the time she hooked up with old Barkley. I say we start there," Trevor suggested.

"Okay, but we need a cover. We don't want rumors about our little search alerting the wrong person."

Trevor agreed. "We could use the school paper approach. We could say we're writing a paper on the town, focusing primarily on its' long-term residents and businesses. Cutter's Cove Market has been here since the thirties. It should qualify."

"That's a good idea. We'll see whose working today and wing it once we get started."

The place was fairly deserted, which was surprising considering the time of day. The only employee visible was a checker, leaning against the counter reading a magazine. They walked over, introduced themselves, and explained their mission.

"Only lived here about five years myself," the checker explained. "Not much of a history buff, so I probably can't tell you much about the place before that. The owner, Mr. Sheldon, might be more helpful, but he's gone for the day. He took the store over from his dad, so he's been around forever. He left early to go on a fishing trip. He should be back in a few days. If he calls in I'll tell him you were looking for him."

"Thank you for your time," Alyson said as they turned to walk away.

"You know who you should talk to?" the clerk added as they neared the door.

"Who?" Alyson stopped and turned around.

"Old Mr. Wilson. He retired a couple of years ago, but he worked here as a janitor for about a hundred years before that."

"Do you know his first name, or have a number where we can reach him?" Trevor asked.

"His name is Ben. Don't know his number, but I'd venture to say he's in the book. Lives over off First somewhere."

"You don't happen to have a phone book we can borrow?" Trevor asked, gifting the middle-aged woman with one of his famous to-die-for smiles.

"Sure, come on back to the office. Maybe your friend could keep an eye out for any customers who might wander in."

"Sure thing." Alyson smiled. Trevor should be ashamed of himself, flirting with the poor woman like that. Of course it probably made her day.

Alyson looked around the store while she waited for Trevor to return. Unlike the specialty markets she was familiar with, this one seemed to contain a little bit of everything. There were your usual canned and boxed goods, fresh meat and seafood counters, an assortment of baked goods bearing the name of the bakery on the wharf, and a good selection of dairy products. There was a pharmacy in the corner, and a section of the store offered basic clothing products like jeans, sweatshirts, socks, and T-shirts. You could even buy a sturdy pair of work boots or nonname-brand tennis shoes. Next to the shoes there were several counters packed with hardware items and household necessities, and the entire back corner was filled with hunting, fishing, and camping supplies. The store was reminiscent of the one-stop trading posts featured in the few westerns she'd seen.

Alyson walked back to the front of the store to check out the candy counter, which prominently displayed an extensive selection. She was seriously considering splurging on some of the locally made chocolates when she heard Trevor returning from the office at the back.

"Thanks again for your time." Trevor smiled once more at the woman as he walked toward Alyson with a slip of paper in his hand.

"Come on back now," the clerk cooed.

"You're really a piece of work," Alyson accused as Trevor grabbed her by the hand and dragged her toward the door. "Playing with that poor woman's emotions like that."

"I got the number, though." He held up the piece of paper triumphantly. "Actually, better than the number. Gladys let me use the phone. I called old Ben and he said we could come on over."

"Right now?"

"Right now. He said he put out some tea and cookies and we could have a nice visit. He sounded lonely," Trevor added as they drove toward First Street.

"I'm impressed. You really know how to take care of business. I'd probably have just taken the number and called tomorrow or something. Of course if you weren't such a pretty boy we might not have got the number at all."

"Don't you start too. I hate it when Mac calls me that."

"Why? Is it an affront to your masculinity or something?"

"Something like that." Trevor looked down at the note in his hand. "Here's the house. Are we sticking to our school paper strategy?"

"Yeah, for now," Alyson confirmed as they walked up the three short steps leading to the porch and rang the bell.

"Come in. Come in," a jolly little man greeted them. "My, aren't you a pretty little thing." He gently grabbed Alyson by the chin to get a better look at her face.

"We'd like to ask you a few questions about the town, the store, and their history, if you don't mind," Trevor said.

"Sure. Sure. I'd love to." The old man started walking toward the back of the house. "I've set out tea and cookies. We'll have a nice long chat, shall we?"

For the first half hour or so they asked the man about the history of the town and the market to avoid drawing undo attention to what really interested them. Alyson took notes during the conversation, in keeping with their school paper cover.

"My dad grew up here and remembered a woman by the name of Mary Swanson who used to work here in the early 1960s," Trevor lied.

Alyson crossed her fingers for good measure.

"Let's see." The old man put his hand to his chin in thought. "There was a pretty little thing named Mary who worked at the store for a spell, but I think it was about ten years before that. If memory serves, she probably would have been gone by the sixties. Cute little thing. Too bad what happened to her."

"Something happened to her?" Trevor prodded.

"Went and got herself pregnant. Never did say who the father was. Back then young women didn't have babies out of wedlock. She was fired as soon as the boss found out. Don't know how she managed all on her own with no job and a baby to raise. I saw her around a few times right after the boy was born, but then she sort of disappeared. I figured she moved on to a town where people didn't know about her embarrassment."

"Do you have any idea where she might have gone?" Alyson asked.

"No clue. Never saw her again."

The pair asked a few more general questions about other past employees, then thanked the man for his hospitality and promised to come back sometime at his repeated insistence.

"You think Mary's baby could be Barkley's child?" Alyson asked as they drove back toward the center of town.

"Dates seem right," Trevor agreed.

"Poor thing. I hadn't even stopped to think about the fact that she would have been ostracized. Single women have babies all the time now and no one thinks much about it."

"It was a different world back then," Trevor sympathized. "There's a pretty good diner around the corner. Want to grab a bite? I'm starving."

"Sure," Alyson agreed. She'd told her mom she was eating in town, so it wouldn't do much for her cover story if she went home and pigged out.

"They have the best meat loaf and mashed potatoes with gravy here. It's truly a work of art."

"I think I'll stick to something a little lighter, but you go ahead."

The café was warm and cozy, with red checked tablecloths, flickering candles, and soft lighting. All of a sudden this started to feel like a date, and although Alyson liked Trevor a lot, she wasn't sure she wanted to go down that particular road with him.

"I'll pay," Alyson insisted, trying to break the normal date routine. "After all, I owe you after you spent the whole weekend helping me clean my attic."

"Sure, whatever," Trevor responded, as if he didn't care one way or the other. "The fog's rolling in and it's getting a little chilly. There's a seat by the fireplace. Let's grab it."

As promised, the food was wonderful. Alyson decided on grilled salmon with dill sauce and Trevor ordered the predicted meat loaf. During dinner the conversation turned to more general subjects like football and classes.

"Excuse me, miss," the waitress interrupted a lively debate about which professional football team was best positioned to win that year's Super Bowl. "The man over by the front door asked me to give this to you."

"What man?" Alyson took the folded slip of paper the waitress handed her and looked toward the door.

"Why, that man in the coat." The waitress turned toward the empty doorway. "He was there a minute ago. I was sitting behind the cashier's counter when he came in, handed me the note, and asked me to give it to you. I guess he must have gone."

Trevor took the note from Alyson. "What exactly did the man look like?" he demanded as he read the note.

"Tall, dark hair. He wore a long coat and a large hat. Sort of looked like one of those detectives in the movies."

"What exactly did he say?" Trevor stood up and walked over to the now empty doorway and looked outside.

"He just asked me to give the note to the young lady at this table." The waitress followed Trevor across the room.

"What is it?" Alyson asked as she joined him on the sidewalk in front of the diner. "What does it say?"

"Get your coat. We're leaving." Trevor handed the waitress a couple of ten-dollar bills to cover their meal.

Following Alyson inside, he grabbed a notepad from the cashier's counter and jotted down his name and cell phone number. "If this guy comes in here again see if you can get his name, then give me a call at this number. It's very important we find out who he is."

"Okay, sure."

Trevor grabbed Alyson's hand and started walking quickly toward the car.

"What is it? What did the note say?"

"Get in. I'll tell you on the way home."

"Trevor, you're scaring me." Alyson buckled her seat belt as Trevor gunned the engine and sped toward her house.

"The note is a warning." Trevor handed it to her.

The note was written in red ink. It said *Mind your own business or suffer the consequences.*

Alyson read the note again, then glanced at Trevor. "Who do you think wrote it?"

"My best guess is that someone doesn't want us to find Barkley's heir. I think we should go to the cops," Trevor said.

"No! I mean, I really don't think that's necessary. If this guy is willing to risk public exposure to give me a note we must be getting close. I really want to solve this mystery. If we go to the police that will pretty much put an end to our investigation."

"But your life might be in danger. Let's not forget about the break-in. I think continuing with our own search might be dangerous. I'm sure the cops will follow up on the information we've uncovered so far."

"Trevor, please. I really want to finish this. I'll be careful. I promise."

"Okay," Trevor reluctantly agreed, "we won't do anything tonight, but you have to tell your mom about everything that's going on, including the note."

"Okay, I will. I wonder how this guy even knows we've been looking for an heir. I mean, we haven't told anyone what we're doing."

"Whoever broke in the other day must have been watching us. He must have found out we talked to Ben Wilson. We must be getting close. Be sure to lock the house up tight and keep your cell phone by your bed. If you hear anything—anything at all, the slightest little noise—you call me, no matter what time it is."

"Okay."

"Promise me."

"I promise."

"Okay, I'll see you tomorrow. And remember, talk to your mom."

Alyson got out of Trevor's car and let herself into the darkened house. Her mom had been working hard and must have already gone to bed. Tomorrow would be soon enough to talk to her.

Chapter 9

"So, how's your studio coming along?" Alyson asked the next morning as she devoured the stack of pancakes her mom had set before her.

"Actually, I haven't even started working on it. The contractor I hired to fix the attic stairs said he'd give me a quote on putting in some large picture windows. He hasn't gotten back to me yet. Besides, I really wanted to get the bedrooms done first."

"I peeked into your room earlier. I love the way you did the curtains. Where'd you ever get the idea to drape them that way?"

"I've seen paintings from around the turn of the century with drapes hung in a similar fashion. I figured because we seem to have purchased such a majestic old house, we might as well decorate it in a way that honors its heritage." Her mom poured an extra dollop of syrup over the remaining pancakes on her plate. "When I first started on the bedrooms I just wanted to make them somewhat livable, but now I'm really excited about decorating the rest of the house. Maybe we should work on clearing out the rest of the downstairs rooms this weekend. I spent part of the afternoon drawing some sketches of what each room might eventually look like and I can't wait to get started."

Alyson was happy to see her mom really getting in to the remodel project. Her face glowed as she continued to share her ideas for each room. It had been a long time since Alyson had seen her mother so happy, so long since her smile had reached her eyes the way it always had before the murder. So much had happened in the past year. For the first time in many months, Alyson felt she could see the first rays of light breaking through the darkness that had become their lives.

". . . and after thinking about it, I decided earth tones with blue accents really would be best."

"Sounds great, Mom." Alyson realized she'd totally missed half of what her mom had said. "I'd better get to school. I'll ask the gang if they can help out again on Saturday. There's some pretty heavy-looking furniture in the bedroom off the kitchen."

"I'm so glad you've made such good friends so quickly. I never did ask how your dinner was last night."

Alyson hesitated. She'd promised Trevor, but her mom seemed so happy. She hated to ruin the mood. "It was great. We went to a cute little café downtown. They had really good food and a warm, cozy atmosphere. It felt like a real hometown locals' place. The kind where, eventually, everyone knows your name."

"We'll have to try it sometime soon; maybe one night later this week. I've been so busy with the remodel I haven't been in cooking mode, the past few days anyway."

"Sure, whenever." Alyson kissed her mom on the cheek as she got out of the car in front of the school.

"Should I pick you up at three, or are you doing something with your friends?"

"I'm not sure yet. Is it okay if I call to let you know?"

"Call my cell. I'll keep it with me because I might not hear the downstairs phone ring if I'm working upstairs."

"Okay, have a good day," Alyson called.

Alyson hurried toward her first-period class, anxious to get some feedback from Mac on her computer search the day before. As with the previous morning, Chelsea was already seated at the table next to Trevor, so she guessed her inquiry would have to wait.

"So how 'bout it, Trev?" Chelsea was asking as Alyson sat down next to Mac.

"Chelsea wants to ride along with us to the dance on Saturday," Mac filled Alyson in.

"Sure, why not?" Trevor answered.

Alyson wasn't sure why Trevor didn't tell Chelsea to buzz off instead of letting her push him around all the time, but it really wasn't her problem and she had more important things to think about.

As with the previous morning, the time until lunch both flew by and dragged on interminably. As soon as the bell sounded, indicating the conclusion of fourth period and the beginning of lunch, Alyson grabbed Mac's arm and hurried her toward the cafeteria.

"I thought fourth period would never end. I've been dying to tell you about our research in town yesterday," Alyson began. "This no-sharing-information-until-lunch thing is killing me."

"I know what you mean," Mac sympathized, "But it's only fair we share information when everyone is together."

"Yeah, I get it. If I was the odd man out I wouldn't want everyone else sharing info without me. Eli's been a huge help and deserves to be in on the conversation. It's just that patience has never been one of my virtues. Every time I try to be patient, I get tired of waiting and my good intentions fly right out the window. I usually end up doing something stupid or saying something out of turn."

"Don't worry." Mac laughed, setting her lunch tray on the table already occupied by Trevor and Eli. "I'll help you keep your virtue intact."

"What's this about virtue?" Trevor asked, suddenly interested in their conversation.

"Wouldn't you like to know?" Mac teased.

"So can we talk about our research yesterday?" Alyson interrupted, anxious to get right to the point.

"Did you talk to your mom?" Trevor asked.

"Uh, not yet. She was asleep by the time I got home last night, and the timing didn't seem right this morning," Alyson answered.

"You promised," Trevor reminded her.

"I know. I will."

"Talk to your mom about what?" Mac asked.

Trevor filled Mac and Eli in on the note, the man who'd left it, and his opinion that Alyson should go to the cops.

"I have to agree with Trevor," Mac responded. "I think you should go to the cops. You could be in real danger. If the guy with the note is the same person who broke in the other day he knows where you live."

"I appreciate everyone's concern, but I'd really like us to continue to pursue this on our own, at least for now," Alyson insisted. "If we go to the cops they'll probably put it on a back burner. We really don't have any proof at all there even is an heir."

"I guess that's true," Mac acknowledged.

"Did you guys find out anything yesterday that might help us prove our theory?" Eli asked.

Alyson filled the other two in on her and Trevor's findings from the previous afternoon. "Of course we have no way of knowing for sure if Mary's baby is Barkley's illegitimate child, or where she might be now, but it's a start."

"I think our research can fill in a few blanks," Mac interjected when Alyson finally stopped to take a breath. "I didn't find a record anywhere of a child born to Mary Swanson. I did a pretty thorough records search from the local hospital, along with all other facilities within a hundred-mile radius. I also checked the county records to see if there was a birth certificate for any babies with the last name of Swanson or Cutter for the years between 1950 and 1970. Again, I drew a blank." Mac leaned forward to emphasize her next point. "I did, however, find a death certificate for Mary Swanson issued in 1968."

"The year the checks stopped," Trevor observed.

"If Mary died, what happened to her child?" Alyson asked.

"I have no idea," Mac said. "I tried to see if I could find any evidence of a child, but there are no records at all of anyone around the presumed age of the child in question with the last name of Swanson."

"We checked school records, medical records, records for this county and the next one over, but we drew a complete blank," Eli added.

"But Ben confirmed Mary did indeed have a child, so why the lack of a paper trail?" Trevor asked.

"He did say she moved away. Maybe she moved out of the area completely," Alyson ventured.

"Is there any way to find out which bank the deductions from Barkley's account were deposited into?" Trevor asked. "That might give us some indication of where she ended up."

"Should be doable," Mac answered. "After quite a few hours of surfing using Eli's dad's software, we managed to find out that the deposits into Barkley's account came from a trust established at a bank in Portland. What's even more interesting is that the deductions are still being drafted from the bank but haven't been deposited in Barkley's local account since he died."

"So where's the money going?" Trevor picked up a potato chip and plopped it into his mouth. "Sounds like someone might be getting rich off of old Barkley's money. Seems to me that might be a pretty good reason for someone not to want a legitimate heir to be found."

"We didn't get that far, but Eli's dad is gone all week, so we have time to work on it. We could look into the transaction from Barkley's account into Mary's at the same time."

"I can check with some of my cyber buddies to see if any of them can give us additional ideas of things to try." Eli took the first bite of his ham sandwich.

"We don't want anyone else to know what we're doing," Alyson cautioned.

"Don't worry; I'll pose the question in a roundabout way without including any specifics. Besides, no one in my chat room knows who anyone else really is. We all have screen names and made-up identities."

"Still," Alyson said, "it seems chat buddies with the level of expertise we're talking about probably have a way of getting around the whole secret screen name thing. There must be a way to trace an online identity to its owner if you know what you're doing."

"I'm sure there probably is, but the computers in our house are equipped with state-of-the-art security software that hasn't even hit the market yet. No one's getting past my dad's security system, I promise."

"Okay." Alyson relaxed. "So let's review our strategy. Mac is going to follow up on the bank accounts to see if she can identify the source and destination of any transactions related to Mary or Barkley's account in general. It would be interesting to know who originally set up the trust and who's been controlling it since Barkley died. Someone or some institution must have become the appointed executor in the absence of any known heirs."

"And what about Barkley's local account?" Eli inquired. "If ten thousand dollars a month was deposited into it for let's say eighty years, there must be a huge balance. It seems he lived fairly frugally."

"That's true." Alyson hadn't considered that. "The bank ledger I found listed a series of transactions, but no beginning or ending balances. I didn't have time to do a thorough search, but the only deductions I came across, other than a few hundred dollars a month for utilities and supplies from the market, were the deposits into Mary's account, and those only lasted for thirteen years. I'll check further tonight."

"I can search the archives of the local newspaper to see if I can come up with any old articles relating to Mary," Eli volunteered. "Even if there isn't a birth announcement, there might be an obituary. Do you want to come by later to help out?" Eli asked Trevor.

"Actually, I may have found Alyson a puppy. How about it, Aly? Want to go check him out this afternoon?"

"Really? What kind of puppy?"

"He's a ten-month-old champion-bred German shepherd. The family of a guy in my history class breeds them. They have a pup they were holding for someone on the East Coast, but the deal fell through for some reason, and the dog's available. He's already been house and basic obedience trained, which is a bonus. He's also going to be huge, and his father is a working police dog, so hopefully the pup will have inherited his daddy's protective instincts. After last night I'll feel a lot better if you have a big ferocious dog in the house. I can take you over to see him after school if you want."

"I'd love to. Do you want to come along, Mac?"

"Why not? It'll be fun. Who doesn't welcome a chance to play with puppies?"

Alyson called her mom before going to PE to confirm that it was still okay if she got a puppy. After getting her mom's approval she arranged to meet Trevor in the parking lot after computer class because Trevor didn't have football practice that day. Mac decided it would be easiest to pick her up from her computer internship on the way out to see the pup. As far as Alyson was concerned, three o'clock couldn't get there soon enough.

The ride out to Trevor's friend's house only took about ten minutes, but Alyson asked three times if they were almost there.

"You really *don't* have much patience," Mac commented after the third inquiry.

"Sorry." Alyson snapped her gum. "I'm just superexcited." She fidgeted in her seat. "I didn't think I would be. I mean, at least not this excited." She snapped her gum again and twirled her hair around her finger for the hundredth time. "Before you suggested I get one, I didn't even know I wanted a dog." She turned to stare out the window. "Weird, huh?"

They arrived at their destination before Alyson wore a hole in Trevor's seat with all her squirming around. "This is Tucker," Trevor introduced her to the dark-haired boy who greeted them. "This is Alyson and Mac," he added, gesturing to each in turn. "Alyson's the one interested in the pup."

"Good to meet you both," Tucker said. "The pup's in the house." He led the way toward a very neat, white ranch-style farmhouse with dark green shutters.

"Tucker," he called after walking into the house.

"You named your dog after yourself?" Alyson questioned.

"My brother did," Tucker responded, as Tucker the dog bounded energetically into the room. "As a pup, Tucker tended to be the most boisterous of the litter, barking incessantly at anything that moved. One day my brother said, 'that dog's always sounding off, just like Tucker,' and unfortunately, in spite of my best attempts to the contrary, the name stuck."

While Tucker was speaking, the pup momentarily paused, then bounded right over to Alyson and sat docilely at her feet, leaning against her leg as if to say *I love you.*

"Wow," Tucker commented. "He really likes you. He doesn't usually run right up to new people that way."

"He's adorable." Alyson vigorously scratched Tucker behind the ears.

"Look at his face." Mac laughed. "His eyes are rolled up in his head like he's in complete ecstasy."

"I think we have a match," Trevor exclaimed. "How about it, Alyson? Want to take this pup home?"

"Definitely." Alyson stopped petting Tucker the pup and turned to Tucker the person. "What do I need to do?"

"Follow me and I'll get you all set up."

After getting a list of directions, shot records, and AKC paperwork, Alyson wrote Tucker a check and loaded her new best friend into the back of Trevor's car.

"He's so cute, and so big." Mac turned in her seat to watch the puppy in the back. "My mom doesn't like dogs. I have a fish, but it's not the same."

"Want to come over and help me get him settled in?" Alyson invited. "You could stay for dinner."

"Sounds like fun. I could help you go through the rest of the paperwork too."

"Talk to your mom," Trevor reminded her as he dropped the girls off at Mac's car. "I have this really bad feeling we're going to regret not going to the cops. Money—especially large sums of money—can make people do things they might not otherwise even consider. Seriously, talk to your mom."

"I will." Alyson leaned over and kissed Trevor on the cheek. "Thanks for finding the puppy for me. I feel safer already. I'll be fine. Really."

"Mom, we're home," Alyson called loudly up the stairs toward the attic.

"Be right down," a faint voice called back

"You guys really need an intercom system," Mac observed.

"Tell me about it."

While the girls were discussing the communication challenges of living in such a large house, Tucker walked around the kitchen, sniffing every nook and cranny. After a thorough search, he settled down on the rug in front of the large, old-fashioned fireplace that took up nearly the entire wall separating the kitchen from the formal dining room.

"Looks like he's settled right in," Mac observed. "He picked a good spot too. It'll be nice and warm during the long winter months."

"I can't wait to have a fire. This house has nine fireplaces." Alyson walked over to pet the newest addition to the family.

"Nine fireplaces? That's a lot."

"I'm pretty sure they were the only source of heat when the house was first built. There are three on each floor. There's one in each of the bedrooms, plus one each in the living room, dining room, and kitchen. Actually, the only main room without a fireplace is the bedroom off the kitchen. I guess the maid didn't warrant any heating."

"Does the house have another heating system now?"

"Sort of. Someone installed a system on the first floor, but it doesn't look like it's worked in years. We're going to install a whole new system as part of our remodel. In the meantime we bought a load of wood for the fireplaces."

"Sounds like a lot of work."

"Tell me about it," Alyson repeated. "So, do you think Tucker's hungry?" she asked, quickly changing the subject back to her new puppy.

"Maybe; it's close to dinner time. I bet he could use some water for sure. He's been panting ever since we picked him up."

"Tucker gave me some food to get me going until I could get to the store. I think there are some metal bowls in one of these cabinets." Alyson began opening and closing cupboard doors, looking for the bowls in question.

"The house is really coming together," Mac observed, looking around as Alyson continued her search. "And this kitchen is awesome. I meant to mention the other day how much I like the way your mom blended the colors and shades in the new cabinets, countertops, paint, and curtains to match the existing colors in the brick fireplace and wood floor. You don't get the feeling you do with some remodels, where the new clashes with the old. The room feels fresh and welcoming without losing its warmth and charm. "

"My mom's an artist. She has a natural flare for texture and color. She's doing the whole house with tones found in the earth and sea. I can't wait to show you my room now that she's finished. It's done in blues and grays, the natural colors of the ocean."

"Sounds cool. Plus a bonus for imitating the school colors."

"I hadn't even thought of that." Alyson laughed. "I guess no one can question my commitment to school spirit."

Tucker bounded across the room to greet Alyson's mom, who had finally made it down from the attic.

"This is Tucker," Alyson introduced.

Mom knelt in front of the pup, who began to thump his tail hard against the floor.

"He's beautiful." She scratched him under the chin. Tucker licked Alyson's mom's hand in greeting. "He seems pretty mellow. I hope he'll make a good watchdog."

"The breeder assured me he's been trained to be mellow when indoors but, if needed, can be quite an aggressive watchdog."

"Well, he's certainly going to be a big dog," her mother stated. "I guess when you said you were getting a puppy I pictured something lap size. He's already bigger than most full-grown dogs."

"He's going to weigh around a hundred pounds," Alyson confirmed. "I was going to get him some food and water. Do you happen to remember where those two large metal bowls ended up?"

"Check the cabinet to the left of the sink."

"Score!" Alyson exclaimed, finding the sought-after bowls toward the back of the cabinet.

"I was just telling Alyson how much I loved what you've done with the kitchen," Mac said. "It has a real traditional country kitchen feel."

"Thanks; I like the way it turned out. I didn't realize how much fun it would be to remodel this old house. At first I viewed it as a chore to be completed, but once I got started the artist in me took over, and I've had the best time."

"I've asked Mac to stay for dinner. I hope that's okay."

"Sure. I was planning on making seafood chowder. I stopped at the outdoor seafood counter on the wharf on my way home from taking you to school and picked up some shrimp, scallops, and lobster. I thought I'd cook them in a light cream sauce along with some diced-up potatoes, carrots, and onion."

"It sounds delicious." Mac rubbed her stomach. "My mom's idea of chowder comes from a can marked Campbell's."

"Not everyone has the time or desire to go to all the effort of creating things from scratch when you can just as easily get them from a can," Alyson's mom commented. "I'm sure your mom has lots of other things she enjoys and is good at."

"I suppose," Mac agreed doubtfully.

"Dinner should be ready in about an hour and a half," she informed the pair. "You can have a snack if you're starving."

"We're fine," Alyson said. "I think we'll go up to my room. Just give a yell when dinner's ready."

Alyson and Mac started up the stairs to the second floor, and Tucker got up to follow them.

"Wow, your room is fantastic! I can't believe it's the same room I saw last week." Mac toured the room, then looked out the window to the view beyond. "It's so strange. I've known that this house was sitting up here on the cliff my whole life, but not once has it occurred to me how cool it would be to live here. When you first mentioned your mom bought this place, I thought both of you were crazy. But now I have to admit I'm a little envious. The house is really going to be great."

Tucker quietly sniffed every corner of Alyson's bedroom as the girls talked, eventually settling down on the large hooked rug next to the bed. He laid his head on his front legs and watched them as they talked and walked around the room.

"Maybe we should start going through those boxes while we're waiting for dinner," Mac suggested, indicating the boxes from the attic, which Alyson had stacked up next to the far wall.

Alyson picked up a box at the top of the pile. "This is the one where I found the check register. I'll keep looking through it. Just pick one of the others and we'll get started."

The girls sat cross-legged on the bed, sorting through their boxes as Tucker watched from the floor. Alyson hadn't known how much she'd missed just sitting in a room and working alongside someone you considered to be your best friend. She'd been friends with Tiffany forever. The two of them had grown up together and had talked often about living together and sitting on a porch in matching rocking chairs after whoever they decided to marry had long since died. Alyson wasn't certain why both she and Tiffany were convinced they'd outlive their spouses, but she guessed that because they'd begun their lives as constant companions, it was only right that they end up the same way.

It made Alyson sad that that would never happen. She'd loved Tiffany more than she'd ever loved anyone other than her mother. She wondered if Tiff had reserved side-by-side rocking chairs for the two of them in heaven.

"Look at what I found." Mac held up a fistful of black-and-white photographs. "They look really old."

Alyson blinked away a tear and leaned in closer to get a better look. "Is there any writing on them to indicate who they might be?"

"No." Mac turned over the photos to look at the backs. "This one has a date on it. Nineteen twenty-two."

"Wow, that's old." Alyson took the photo from Mac and studied the middle-aged man holding a young boy who appeared to be around two. "Do you think this is Barkley and his dad?"

"Could be. The date seems about right."

Alyson continued to study the pair in the photo. "If it is, it's sad to think about what eventually happened to them. They look so happy."

"Here's another one with writing on it." Mac held up a photo of a baby boy lying on some type of blanket. "It just says Jonathan. No date."

"The quality of the film looks a little better. I would guess it's a more recent photo than the first one. See if you can find any other photos with the same people in them, or any photos with writing on them."

Mac sorted through the box while Alyson continued to study the check ledger.

"Look at this," Alyson said after several minutes. "There's a one-time cash withdrawal from the account in August of 1955 for twenty-five thousand dollars."

"Just before the payments to Mary started. Do you think it was a down payment of some type?"

"Maybe. Or maybe it was a payment to a doctor or midwife; someone who would have quietly assisted with the birth."

"Makes sense. That might account for the lack of official records. Maybe the baby was delivered at home under a veil of secrecy."

"It's too bad there's no name here. It would have been helpful to have another lead to follow up on."

"We could ask around town to see if anyone remembers who the town doctor was, or if there was a midwife working at the time," Mac suggested. "It was a long time ago, but there are several residents who were around back then."

"Good idea." Alyson continued to sort through the box in front of her. "I wish I could find the early ledgers. So far I haven't found anything dated before 1945. Can you imagine how much ten thousand dollars was worth in 1945?"

"You're right; I hadn't thought of that." Mac stopped to consider the implications. "My grandparents were married in 1933 and my grandmother once told me she and my grandpa paid three thousand dollars for their first house. If Barkley was given ten thousand dollars a month from the start that would have been a fortune."

"It makes sense. If we assume Barkley's father set up the trust in the first place, the payments would either have started with his death or maybe when Barkley reached adulthood."

"When did we decide his father must have died?" Mac asked.

"Must have been sometime between 1930 and 1940."

"Maybe the payments didn't start until he was older and 1945 is the beginning date," Mac ventured.

"Could be, but I'll keep looking just in case. Maybe the early documents, if there are any, are in another box." Alyson returned the papers to the first box and placed it on the floor next to the others, then picked up another. When she picked up that box a single sheet of paper fluttered to the floor. "That's strange."

"Maybe Barkley is trying to tell us something."

"Maybe. I told you about the gust of wind that revealed the check ledger with the payments to Mary Swanson." Alyson held up the single piece of yellowed paper. "I wonder what it means."

"It looks like some kind of code."

"Do you have any idea how to read it?"

"Not off hand, but if you want I'll take it with me and work on it. Basically, it's just the alphabet arranged in box format. Five letters over and five letters down, with *i* and *j* sharing a single space. There's a series of numbers next to that."

Alyson studied the diagram but couldn't make out any patterns offhand. Maybe Mac and her super brain could figure it out.

a	b	c	d	e
f	g	h	ij	k
l	m	n	o	p
q	r	s	t	u
v	w	x	y	z

44	23	15	14	15	11	14	32	11	33	22	45	11
42	14	43	44	23	15	43	15	13	42	15	44	
44	23	15	14	15	11	14	32	11	33	31	24	15
43	34	33	44	23	15	35	11	44	23	34	21	35
24	42	11	44	15	43							
43	15	51	15	33	44	54	52	15	43	44	21	34
45	42	15	24	22	23	44	54	44	53	34	33	34
42	44	23										

"Dinner's ready," Alyson's mom called from downstairs.

"Coming," Alyson replied. "I guess this will have to wait. I'm starved."

"I'll take it home and run it through the computer," Mac said. "It's probably some sort of cipher or code."

Dinner was delicious, as promised. Tucker quietly chowed down on puppy food, while the others enjoyed the thick, rich chowder. The conversation centered on Tucker and his exercise and training needs. It was decided Alyson would walk him every morning before school and her mother would try to take him out around lunchtime. Alyson planned to run him every afternoon before it got dark so he'd have a chance to get all his puppy energy out before settling in for the night. And she planned to ask Tucker the breeder's son if she could pay his dad to continue with the dog's training a couple of days a week because neither she nor her mom had any idea about how to proceed.

"I'll take him out after dinner," Alyson added. "It'll be dark in a couple of hours."

Alyson and Mac took Tucker for a run along the cliffs overlooking the crashing waves. "Do you think it's true that Barkley walked these cliffs at night?" Mac shouted over the thunder of the waves crashing on the rocks below the bluff.

"Makes sense. He didn't want to be seen by anyone for some reason, and he must have needed at least some exercise and fresh air. What better place to walk than along deserted cliffs at night?"

"Sounds lonely," Mac observed. "And a little scary. It can get pretty dark out here, especially when the fog rolls in. He might have fallen to his death in the darkness."

Alyson shrugged. "I'm sure he knew his way around. He lived here his entire life and never went anywhere else." She wrapped her sweater more tightly around her body as the chill from the damp air began to seep in.

The tide had come in during the past hour, which caused the surf to morph from a gently rolling tide to giant waves. Sometimes at night Alyson would lay awake and listen to the echo of the waves as they made their way through the nearby canyon.

"It looks like Tucker is having fun." Alyson watched his playful puppy antics with a smile. "He hasn't stopped running since we started walking." The puppy bounded through the tall brown grass as he chased what Alyson imagined were grasshoppers.

"Looks like he's cornered a rabbit or something," Mac said as Tucker stopped running but continued to bark vigorously at something near a thick growth of vines near the edge of the cliff.

"Tucker," Alyson called to the barking dog. He immediately stopped, looked up at her, and came running back.

"Good boy," she praised him. "He really is well-trained, just like Tucker the human promised."

Tucker continued to sit at her feet, but she could hear him whining under his breath as he stared at the thicket near the cliff.

"I'm sure if he trapped a rabbit it's long gone by now. We should probably get back. I'd like to have time to work on the cipher after I finish my homework. Besides, you need to have a nice long chat with your mother. Trevor is right; you might be in danger. You really need to let her know what's going on."

"I will. I promise."

Mac looked at her skeptically.

"I will. Tonight. Geez, having you and Trevor for friends is like having two extra mothers."

Alyson stopped walking and reached out to hug her new friend with all the pent-up emotion she'd wanted to deliver to Tiffany these past months. Mac seemed startled at first, but then she hugged Alyson back as long and hard as Alyson longed for.

"Thank you for your concern." Alyson eventually pulled back. "I'll talk to my mom. I promise."

After Mac left Alyson sat down with her mom and filled her in on everything that was going on, including the note. It wasn't an easy conversation to have; the last thing Alyson wanted to do was to put her mom through any more worry and pain than she already had. Of all the people she had once had in her life, her mom was the only one who remained.

"You could really be in danger. Maybe you should just drop the whole thing," she suggested.

"Mom, the last thing I want to do is worry you. But now that I know Barkley might have an heir I can't just drop it."

Her mother sat back and looked at Alyson, then tucked a lock of her long blond hair behind her ear. "I understand why this is important to you. I really do. I know you felt helpless to help Tiffany, and this feels like something you and your friends might actually be able to solve. But besides the very real danger you might be in, it worries me that all of this digging around may somehow bring attention to our own situation. We really can't afford to do anything that might make people here start asking a lot of questions about us. We're finally starting to rebuild our lives. I'd hate to see everything we've worked for destroyed."

"I know, Mom. I've thought about that too. But I'm being really careful."

"If someone finds out about us we'll need to leave," Mom warned her.

"No one will."

"What if you get too close to something and the police decide to look into your background?"

"Our cover is really solid," Alyson reminded her mom. "You tell me that every day. Donovan assured us that all of the background and documentation we would need was in place. We just have to stick to our story. If the local authorities check, they'll find school records for Alyson Prescott at Great Lakes High School and Middle School in Minnesota, Minnesota drivers' licenses and tax returns for Sarah Prescott, and birth certificates and finger print records for both of us bearing our new names. We *are* Sarah and Alyson Prescott now. We just have to remember that."

"I'll call Donovan to see what he thinks," her mother said. "I'd like to have this potential heir found too, but your life is more important to me. There are already enough people in the world who want you dead. I just want you to be safe."

"Mom, we both know that no matter what we do, we'll never be completely safe."

Chapter 10

Alyson joined Mac, Trevor, and Eli at lunch the next day. Taking a lemon yogurt and an apple from her backpack, she sat down next to Mac, who was enjoying a huge plate of the greasiest chili fries Alyson had ever seen. The girl must have a cast-iron stomach.

"I decoded the cipher." Mac jumped right in, pulling out a sheet of paper. "It's a Polybius checkerboard. Basically, each number refers to the row and column where the corresponding letter can be found. The first number, 44, represents four rows down, then four columns over to uncover a T, followed by an H and then an E, to spell the word THE."

"What does it say?" Eli asked.

"The first set, which I determined to be the first two rows, given the empty space at the end of row 2, says *the dead man guards the secret.* The second set, beginning with row 3, says *the dead man lies on the path of pirates.* And the third set, beginning with 43 after the incomplete line, says *seventy west, four eighty-two north.*"

"Okay, what does it mean?" Eli questioned.

"I'm not sure, but I think if we're going to solve this mystery we'll need to figure it out."

"I'm suddenly finding myself hoping Barkley's secret is the identity of an heir, as we thought, and not the cover-up of some gruesome murder." Alyson shuddered.

"I guess the only way we're going to find out is to continue to follow the clues," Mac said. "I've been working on getting through the security system at the bank and was able to trace the money being drawn out of Barkley's account and put into Mary's. It seems the money was being deposited into a bank in Tacoma, Washington."

"That must be where Mary went after she left here," Eli concluded.

Mac licked a dollop of chili from her finger and then wiped her hand on a napkin. She pulled another sheet of paper from her backpack. "I checked the county records and found out Mary married someone named Michael Wellington in November 1956. She divorced him a year later. It occurred to me that maybe she married the guy to give her baby a legitimate name. So I checked the local school records and found a Jonathan Wellington enrolled between 1960 and 1968."

"Jonathan," Alyson interrupted. "That's the name we found on the photograph in Barkley's stuff."

"We know Mary died in 1968," Trevor joined in. "So what happened to Jonathan after that?"

"I have no idea," Mac answered as she nibbled on the end of a French fry. "The paper trail ended, until a couple of years ago."

"What happened then?" Alyson asked impatiently. She didn't know how Mac could think about food at a time like this, let alone keep stuffing her face.

"I did an online search for an obituary for Mary. I didn't find one, but I did find an obituary for a Jonathan Wellington, who died on July 22, 2002."

"Are you sure it's the same Jonathan?" Alyson asked.

"Well, not a hundred percent," Mac admitted, "but the paper did say he was forty-seven years old, so the age matches."

"What else did the obituary say?" Alyson prodded.

"Not a whole lot, except that he left behind a wife and a son named Caleb."

"Did it say how he died?" Trevor asked.

"No, it just gave the date of his death and his surviving relatives."

"So if Jonathan's dead, the missing heir is Caleb," Alyson deduced. "Can we find out anything about Caleb?"

"There's a Caleb Wellington who goes to this school," Trevor informed them. "He's a junior too. A member of the drama club, real artsy."

"Makes sense." Mac nodded. "The article indicated Jonathan lived in Cutter's Cove at the time of his death."

"Do you think he knew he was Barkley's son?" Alyson wondered.

"We don't know for certain he *was* Barkley's son," Mac reminded them. "Our investigation so far seems to indicate he probably was, but we have no hard evidence, like a birth certificate, eyewitnesses, or incriminating letters. And," she continued, "I don't think he could have known about Barkley. Otherwise why wouldn't he have come forward when Barkley died? It looks like the estate is probably worth millions."

"Wait a minute. Now I'm confused. Who died first, Barkley or Jonathan?" Alyson asked.

"Good question," Mac responded. "Hang on and I'll check my notes."

Mac set her plate of chili aside and dug into her backpack. She pulled out a manila file folder, opened it, and pulled out a sheet of lined yellow paper. "Jonathan died on July 22 and Barkley was found dead on August 3 of the same year."

"Wow, that's beyond coincidence." Trevor shook his head. "Both men dying within a couple of weeks of each other."

"Should we talk to Caleb?" Alyson asked.

"Not yet," Mac replied. "We need to see if we can find anything concrete linking Jonathan and Barkley. I mean, it's still feasible Mary got pregnant by someone else and Barkley just befriended her when she delivered his groceries, so he felt sorry for her and decided to help her out financially."

"I doubt it," Alyson said.

"I agree," Mac nodded, "but so far we have tons of speculation and no proof."

"Mac's right," Trevor agreed. "We don't want to suggest to Caleb that he might be the heir to millions and end up being totally wrong. Besides," he added, "we still don't know where the withdrawals from the trust have been going since Barkley's death. If someone doesn't want an heir to be found, we might be putting Caleb in danger."

"It seems we still have more questions than answers," Alyson complained.

The conversation died as the gang finished eating. Alyson looked out the window at the surfers who had decided to take advantage of the unusually large waves. Cutter's Cove was definitely a surfing town where huge waves served as almost an excuse for cutting class or calling in sick to work.

Alyson found that most longtime residents, like Mac and Trevor, took the sensational view the lunchroom provided for granted. But Alyson was sure she'd never tire of the beauty of the sun shining on the clear blue water as waves of various sizes crashed onto the white sand beach.

Alyson returned her attention to the conversation as Trevor broke the silence.

"Have you had any luck at all tracing the destination of the money?" Trevor asked.

"Not so far," Mac responded. "There's an extra layer of protection surrounding this particular transaction, above and beyond the normal security of the bank."

"I almost forgot—Mac and I found a cash withdrawal for twenty-five thousand dollars in August of 1955, and now we know that was a month before Jonathan was born," Alyson volunteered. "We think maybe Barkley used the money to pay a doctor or midwife to help with the delivery but keep things quiet."

"Makes sense," Trevor concurred. "I wonder if there's any way to find out who the recipient of the money might have been."

"We talked about that," Mac answered for both of them. "Maybe there's someone in town who knows who would have been qualified to deliver babies at around that time."

"Who would most likely know the entire story behind the birth of Mary's baby," Eli added.

"This could be the break we've been looking for," Trevor concluded.

"Wow, check us out." Alyson offered her hand to the group in a high-five. "Only a few days and we've almost nailed this mystery."

"I think we should meet at my house after football practice and work on the clue from the cipher. If the doctor/midwife thing turns out to be a dead end, it might be the only clue we have to go on," Alyson pointed out.

"Should we bring shovels?" Trevor asked. "That code makes it sound like some type of buried or hidden body might be involved."

"I think we have a couple of shovels in the shed if we need them," Alyson answered.

Mac showed up at Alyson's house at three forty-five, with the guys appearing at three fifty-eight exactly.

"Something smells really good." Eli inhaled deeply as he walked into the kitchen and set his backpack on the floor next to the kitchen table.

"It's the meat sauce for Mom's famous lasagna," Alyson bragged.

"When's dinner? I'm starving." Trevor walked over to the stove to look more closely at the simmering pot of meat sauce.

"Not for a while yet. Don't worry; I knew you'd be hungry, so I set out a snack." Alyson pointed to a tray with hunks of cheese, freshly sliced salami, fruit, and crackers. "Don't get filled up, though. You won't want to spoil your dinner. Trust me: Mom's lasagna is legendary."

The group attacked the plate like they hadn't eaten in weeks. Alyson got a kick out of watching her new friends eat. It was nice to be around people who had healthy appetites.

"So, were you able to find anything out about the deaths?" Alyson asked Mac as she nibbled on a piece of cheese.

"According to police records, Jonathan's death was a suicide and Barkley died of natural causes," Mac answered.

"A suicide?" Trevor asked. "Did he shoot himself?"

"No, he died from ingesting a bottle of painkillers."

"Was any kind of investigation done to confirm it was a suicide?" Alyson asked. "I mean, given the circumstances, what proof do the police have that someone else didn't drug him?"

"I guess he left a note." Mac shrugged. "The police seemed to buy the suicide angle and the case was closed before it was ever really opened."

"Was there a copy of the suicide note in his police file?" Alyson asked

"I'm not sure. I didn't specifically look for it, but I will," Mac assured her.

"What if," Trevor speculated, "someone killed Jonathan and made it look like a suicide."

"I don't know how we're going to confirm whether Jonathan was killed if an autopsy wasn't performed at the time," Alyson said.

"Alyson has a point," Mac agreed. "It's going to be hard to prove much of anything unless we can establish a clear motive. What kind of cheese is this? It's delicious."

"Gruyère. Try the Camembert on a cracker. I think you'll like it too."

"I'm a cheddar man myself," Trevor announced.

"I'm not surprised in the least." Alyson smiled fondly.

"Do you think the cops will take another look at the suicide if we can come up with a motive?" Eli moved the conversation back to the mystery at hand.

Mac spread some cheese on a cracker. "Probably not, although it couldn't hurt to ask."

"It seems like the motive has to be the money," Trevor insisted as he shoved a slice of salami into his mouth. "We need to figure out where the money has been routed since Barkley's death."

"After I checked the police records I spent some time working on the security system attached to the phantom bank withdrawals and I think I'm getting close," Mac informed them. "The money is being routed through several different accounts. I think the key to the whole thing lies somewhere with the trust. I wish we could get a look at the original document that established it. It might hold some important clues. I'll work on it some more tonight."

"So about this buried body . . ." Eli, who had mostly been silent prior to this point, changed the subject. "I came ready to dig; are we going to?"

"I think digging is very much a matter of finding something to dig up," Mac commented. "Maybe we should see if we can find something to dig up before we drag a bunch of shovels around. We can always come back for them if we need them." She wiped her hands on a napkin.

"I've been thinking about the cipher." Alyson unfolded the copy of the code she'd slipped into her pocket at lunch. "Seventy west and four eighty-two north must be directions of some type."

"That makes sense," Trevor agreed, "but seventy what? Feet? Miles? Cartwheels? We really need a frame of reference."

"Yeah, and even if we figure that out," Eli added, "how do we know where to start counting?"

"Let's just try something and see what, if anything, we find," Mac suggested. "I think it makes the most sense that seventy and four eighty-two refer to feet, or maybe steps. We know Barkley never left the house, so miles wouldn't make sense, and the guy was pretty old, so I think we can rule out cartwheels."

"Okay, so where do we start?" Trevor asked.

"How about the northwest corner of the house?" Alyson suggested. "If that doesn't lead us anywhere we can pick another starting place and see what we find. It really is going to be like finding a needle in a haystack, but I guess we need to start somewhere."

It was starting to get cool, so they donned their jackets before heading out along the cliff trail, with Tucker leading the way. He ran ahead of them, as if he could guess where they were going. Seventy steps west brought them almost to the edge of the cliff overlooking the ocean. Four eighty-two steps north brought them to the vicinity where Alyson and Mac had walked the day before. Tucker ran straight back to the spot where he'd barked and started to dig.

"Maybe something's buried there," Mac said.

"Like what?" Alyson asked.

"I don't know. Probably a dead animal or something." Mac walked closer to the vigorously digging pup. "It looks like he's found something."

Alyson leaned over to try to see what he'd dug up. "It looks like . . ." Alyson paused and looked up at Mac, "It looks like a human arm."

"What!" Mac exclaimed.

"Tucker, come," Alyson called the dog away from his prize. "Sit. Stay," she commanded. Tucker sat in the spot Alyson indicated as she walked over to examine the find more closely. Moving the dirt aside, she continued to dig with her hands as best she could.

"It doesn't appear there are any other bones," Alyson observed. "Just a hand and an arm. Of course the rest may be buried deeper. Or maybe the rest of the body is somewhere else and the arm was detached and moved."

"It looks like the hand is pointing toward something," Trevor said. "All the fingers are bent inward except the index finger. It looks like it was purposely posed in that position."

"But who would do something like that?" Eli asked.

"Barkley," Alyson and Mac said in unison.

"I wish we had brought a shovel. We need to see if the rest of the body is here." Alyson looked toward the darkening sea. "It's getting dark and the fog's rolling in. We'll have to come back."

"Do you think we should call the police?" Mac asked.

"Probably," Alyson answered. "But I want a chance to look around a little more first. It looks like this arm has been here for a long time. A few more days shouldn't matter."

"Maybe we should take a look around before we disturb the arm by digging around it," Mac suggested. "The arm may be pointing to a very specific spot."

"I hadn't thought of that. Okay," Alyson said, "if you follow the sight line of the index finger you have a cliff face."

"Let's take a closer look at the cliff," Mac said. "Maybe there's a hidden cave or something."

"Should have brought flashlights," Eli added as a thick blanket of moisture began to make its way toward the shoreline.

They spent the next fifteen minutes searching the face of the cliff through the thick undergrowth. The longer they looked around, the colder it became. They really didn't have long before the entire area would be engulfed in the thick clouds that were peeking over the top of the cliff.

"I don't see anything." Trevor stopped to look around. "Maybe the arm just happened to fall that way when it was dumped and it's not really pointing toward anything at all. We really should get back. The visibility is just going to get worse."

"Where's Tucker?" Alyson asked, looking around for the dog.

"He was here a minute ago," Mac said.

"Tucker!" Alyson called.

A bark sounded from somewhere beyond the thick foliage.

"Here, boy," she called again. She felt a moment of panic as the fog grew even closer.

Just then Tucker bounded out from behind the growth, dragging a vine behind him.

"There must be a cave behind the vines," Eli guessed. "The first time he barked it sounded like he was far away."

"We should get back," Alyson said.

"Let's just take quick peek," Trevor said.

They began to tear at the vines, with Tucker barking beside them.

"He thinks this is a game," Trevor observed.

"I think I found something," Mac called to the group. She pulled the remaining tangle of vines away from the rocky face of the cliff to reveal a small hole leading into the rock formation.

"We're definitely going to need flashlights," Eli said. "The entrance is so tiny it can't let much light in."

"Maybe Tucker can help us out," Alyson suggested. "Fetch, boy," she said firmly, pointing toward the opening in the side of the cliff.

Tucker barked and ran into the small hole. He came back a few seconds later with a bone in his mouth that looked suspiciously human.

"Do you think the rest of the body is in there?" Eli asked.

"Probably," Trevor responded. "But why bury the arm out here? Why not bury the whole thing in the cave?"

"Maybe there's something else in there," Alyson ventured. "Or whoever buried the body wanted to be sure someone eventually found it."

"But why not bury the whole thing out here?" Mac repeated.

"Wild animals?" Alyson guessed.

"Maybe the whole skeleton was inside the cave originally and someone moved the arm out here more recently," Trevor speculated.

"Barkley?" Mac guessed.

Trevor looked out toward the fog that was rolling in more quickly now. "It's getting dark. We'll have to come back tomorrow."

Dinner wasn't quite ready when they returned to the house, so they settled into the living room, which contained only lawn furniture. They began several conversations regarding school and the new season's television lineup, but after several failed attempts it seemed obvious everyone was still very much focused on the mystery they hoped to solve.

"Maybe we could use this time to look around for the key to the trunk," Mac suggested.

"How many rooms still have furniture in them that hasn't been gone through yet?" Eli asked.

"There are two rooms on the third floor with stuff still in them, plus the one we stacked all the stuff from the attic into. The rooms mostly have bedroom furniture, but I think I remember seeing a desk in one of them. The rooms on the second floor have all been cleared out," Alyson said. "There are just the two bedrooms my mom and I are using, a bath, and what was probably a third bedroom that my mom plans to use as an office. The bottom floor probably has the most potential. It looks like Barkley pretty much lived on that floor exclusively. The kitchen has been completely gutted and remodeled. It looks like the room we're sitting in must have been used as a living room, and there's another smaller room that was probably a parlor. Just on the other side of that wall is a formal dining room, another bathroom, and a bedroom off the kitchen, which looks like the one Barkley was using."

"If I wanted to hide something valuable I'd keep it close. Let's take a look at the bedroom on this floor," Trevor said.

The room in question held a dresser, a large bed with a saggy, moth-eaten mattress, a large oak desk, two scratched-up nightstands, and a rocking chair that looked like an antique. The closet, as well as the dresser, was stuffed with clothes, boxes, and other personal belongings.

"It feels so dirty in here," Mac said, keeping her arms to her sides. She grimaced as she looked around the room. "Totally creepy. He must have died in that bed."

"The place was a real mess when we moved in," Alyson told them. "We stripped the bed and picked up all the clothes and personal items in plain sight before starting on the kitchen. I think I'm glad I didn't know about the history of the place before we started cleaning up. It definitely would have given me the willies to know I was stripping the bed a man died in, even if it was four years ago."

"What did you do with all the stuff you cleared out of here?" Trevor asked.

"We took it to the dump, but I'd remember if we came across any keys."

The group started opening drawers and emptying things from the closet. An hour's search produced a lot of worthless junk but no keys.

"Man, this closet is packed from floor to ceiling. It looks like old Barkley was a bit of a pack rat."

Trevor was starting to close the door when a shoebox fell off a shelf and onto his foot.

"Look at this," Alyson said, holding up a fistful of old newspaper clippings from the box she'd picked up. "There's an article about Kennedy Elementary School's spring production of *Cinderella*. Jonathan Wellington played the king." Alyson passed the article to Mac. "And here's another one about a spelling bee. Jonathan came in third."

"What else is in the box?" Eli asked.

"It's mainly all newspaper clippings." Alyson continued to sort through the box. "Some of them seem kind of random. Here's a list of baseball scores, and an article about an accident on the interstate."

"Does it say who was involved in the accident?" Mac asked.

"No, it just says that a vehicle traveling in the wrong direction caused a major pileup, killing four people. The names of the victims aren't listed. I wonder if Mary died in a car accident."

"Maybe if I do a more focused search we can find out," Mac said.

Alyson held up a slightly less yellowed article. "This is about Jonathan's suicide."

"So Barkley *did* know Jonathan's fate before he died," Trevor concluded. "I wonder if he knew about Caleb."

"He's mentioned in the article. I think dinner must be about ready. We should get washed up. We can finish sorting through this stuff later."

Chapter 11

Alyson joined the gang at their usual table at lunch the next day. She'd managed to find a fairly innocent-looking turkey sandwich among the cafeteria's more greasy selections.

"I can't believe you eat that stuff," she said, noting the huge hamburger Mac was eating, and the large grease stain on the plate in front of her.

"You should try it. It's really good." Mac licked a dollop of ketchup that was threatening to drip off the bottom of her burger. "Want a bite?"

"No thanks." Alyson shuddered before biting into her sandwich.

"The problem is," Trevor teased, "you approach food like a science. You need to develop a sense of adventure and try new things."

"Trust me, I have more than enough adventure in my life," Alyson assured him.

"Really? Have you ever tried a jalapeño popper?" Trevor asked.

Alyson scrunched up her nose. "No, I can't say that I have."

"Then you, my friend, are in for a treat." Trevor picked up one of his poppers and dipped it in the thick ranch dressing on his plate. "Open up."

"No. I think I'll pass," Alyson insisted.

"Come on. No guts, no glory," Trevor said persuasively.

She smiled. "My mom warned me about peer pressure."

Trevor laughed. "Okay, you win, but you're really missing out." He turned his attention to Mac. "Were you able to spend any more time working on our theory regarding Jonathan Wellington's death?"

"I hacked back into the police records on my laptop after I got home. Can you believe that? My laptop!" Mac sounded outraged. "Our local police really need to tighten up their security system. It wasn't all that hard, and my laptop isn't even half as powerful as the computer I used at Cybertech the first time."

"And you found?"

"There was a mention of the suicide letter in the file, but apparently no one bothered to scan it into the computer. I think the only way we're going to get a look at it is to get our hands on the hard copy. The problem is that as antiquated as the system used by our local law enforcement appears to be, I doubt even they'd let us just waltz into the police station and ask to go through files."

"We need an insider," Alyson said. "Do any of you know any of the local police officers?"

"Not a police officer, but maybe someone who can help us." Eli's eyes lit up.

"Who?" Mac asked.

"My brother Devon."

"You have a brother?" Mac asked. "How come you've never mentioned said brother before this? And why haven't I seen him when I've been over to use your computer?"

"You haven't seen him because Dev's back east with my dad. He's almost as brilliant on the computer as you are. He's helping my dad install the new security system he's been working on."

"Does he work at the police station?" Trevor asked.

"Not really, but he has access to the files. He's helping the county update and computerize all their historical records. He works for the county part-time, when he isn't in school."

"He goes to school here?" Alyson asked.

"Sort of. Dev should have graduated last year, but he missed a lot of time in Seacliff High is letting him finish up here. He just takes two classes in the morning and will graduate in December. He's hoping to start college midyear. Because of the project with my dad, he got permission to miss the first couple of weeks of school. He'll be home tonight. I'll introduce you to him tomorrow. I don't think he's starting classes until Monday, but he should be at the game."

Alyson had arranged to get a ride out to her house with Mac after school. Trevor was going to meet them there after football practice. Eli had promised to pick up his dad and brother at the airport in Portland, so the others promised to call him with their findings that night.

"I've got news," Mac said as soon as she got into her battered yellow Bug. "I was finally able to trace the destination of the money still being drawn from the trust. It was quite a journey, but persistence paid off."

Mac turned onto the dirt road leading out to Alyson's house. "The work I'd already done gave me a good jumping-off point, and I was able to trace the money through the labyrinth of consecutive deposits and withdrawals that have been made. The trail ended with a local corporation, Heritage Industries. I did some digging and found that the president of the company is a vice president at the bank where the transaction trail initially began. His name is Jason Mastin, and it looks like he's been with the bank for a long time, at least twenty years. The corporation was formed the same month Barkley died, and it appears he's been siphoning off the money ever since. He's been routing it through a bunch of different accounts at different financial institutions all over the world. The thing is, though, in the end the money ended up right here in Portland, at the very bank where the journey began."

"You're kidding!" Alyson turned around in her seat to face Mac. "Why hasn't anyone at the bank caught on to him? Surely someone must have noticed that the monthly deductions from the account continued after Barkley's death. And what about whoever is supposed to be in charge of administering the trust on the Cutter family's behalf? Surely they would have noticed."

"That's the thing. I did some more checking and found that the trust was originally drawn up by Barkley's father, Jacob, in 1920. The only thing I could get a look at online was the signature page, so I'm not sure what the terms of the trust were, but we can assume the intention was to provide for Barkley because the date on the original trust document coincides with the year of Barkley's birth."

"Makes sense," Alyson concurred.

Mac pulled up in front of Alyson's house. "The really interesting thing, though, is that the signature page was witnessed by Harold Laslow, a partner in the law firm of Huntington, Laslow, and James. The firm still exists, but none of the original partners still practice."

"They're probably dead. The trust was established eighty-six years ago."

"The managing partner of the firm today is Steven Laslow, Harold's grandson. It appears he's been acting as executor of the trust since Barkley's death."

"So he must be in on it."

"I think so. I Googled both Steven Laslow and Jason Mastin, and it turns out they both went to Berkeley at the same time."

"They've been ripping off Caleb this whole time!" Alyson exploded.

"Well," Mac reminded her, "we still aren't sure Caleb is Barkley's heir, and the only thing we really have is meaningful coincidence. We know an account set up by Jason Mastin's corporation is receiving the monthly deposits, but we don't have a direct tie to the transactions for Steven Laslow."

"There's one thing I don't get. It's not like ten thousand dollars a month is chump change, but assuming both men are in on the scheme, why risk everything for a hundred twenty thousand dollars a year? Steven Laslow is the managing partner in a law firm. I bet he makes ten times that a year. Why take the risk? Even Jason Mastin, as a vice president of a bank, must make six figures."

"I thought of that too. But I don't think they're after the ten thousand dollars a month. I couldn't even find any evidence that the money that was deposited into Jason Mastin's dummy corporation has ever been withdrawn. I think they're after the bulk of the money still being held in the trust. I decided to bone up on my local history, and it seems the Cutter family was quite rich. Jedediah Cutter worked in shipping, and from what I've read he did quite well. There's even speculation among some local historians that he ran a smuggling operation on the side."

"The cave we found yesterday," Alyson speculated. "If it does go down to the ocean that may be how he got his smuggled goods in and out without having to use the docks."

"But the opening was so small."

"It might have been larger originally. There could have been a cave-in at some time in the past. So how much money do you think we're talking about?"

"Possibly tens, maybe even hundreds of millions."

"Wow."

"There's no way to know for sure," Mac concluded, "but it must be a lot if men like Jason Mastin and Steven Laslow are willing to take such a big risk to get to it."

Alyson grabbed the handle next to her and opened the car door but didn't get out. "You'd think that with a pot of money that big the trust would be on lots of people's radar."

"I don't think the money's all in one place. The bank in Portland probably only holds enough to make the deposits into Barkley's account. The rest is probably tied up in other accounts, or even other types of investments. My guess is that originally someone at Huntington, Laslow, and James managed the trust on Barkley's behalf, because he was only ten at the time his father died. Whoever was in charge of administering the trust probably made investment decisions on his behalf. Normally, once the heir reaches the age of maturity he takes control of his money, but let's assume Barkley didn't want to, or wasn't able to, do it. He might have turned the management of the trust over to the law firm permanently."

Mac got out of the car to stretch her legs but continued to speak. "Generations have gone by and the money is spread out into many investments, the way large fortunes are bound to be. Everyone originally involved in the trust is dead, the only apparent heir is dead, no one has come forward claiming any part of the inheritance, so Mastin and Laslow figure that if they help themselves to the Cutter family assets no one will be any the wiser. I mean, technically, if Barkley signed management rights over to Huntington, Laslow, and James, Steven probably has the right to invest the money anywhere he sees fit, even in Heritage Industries. In the absence of anyone to protest, all of the money could eventually be moved into dummy accounts. No one would ever know."

"Are you saying that so far no illegal transactions have taken place?" Alyson asked.

"Not technically, but if we prove Caleb is the heir, he probably could argue conflict of interest regarding at least the Heritage Industries investment."

"It stands to reason, then, that if Jason and Steven are helping themselves to the Cutter family millions they probably don't want an heir found. Do you think one of them is our phantom thief? Whoever broke in to the house that night was definitely looking for something specific."

"Like a will or a birth certificate?" Mac ventured.

"Makes sense, especially if they know about the existence of an heir. They probably figure as long as

Caleb doesn't find out that he's entitled to the money they're in the clear."

"Do you think they'd hurt him?" Mac asked.

"I doubt it, but you never know. We're talking about a lot of money, and it looks like Caleb might be the only person standing in their way. We need to find proof that he's the rightful heir, and fast." Alyson began walking toward the house. "Caleb might not be safe until we have enough proof to go public."

Alyson opened the kitchen door and found Tucker camped out on the rug in front of it. He immediately jumped up and began what Alyson fondly thought of as the dance of the abandoned dog. He circled her feet several times, licked her hand, and wagged his whole body in greeting. Alyson reached down to scratch his neck, and he promptly sat down at her feet.

"You'd think you'd been gone a week." Mac smiled.

"He doesn't seem to have any sense of the passage of time." Alyson responded. "If I'm gone an hour or all day I'm greeted with the same happy dance."

"It's sweet." Mac reached down to pet the dog at Alyson's feet. "My goldfish doesn't miss me at all when I'm gone."

"I'm going to go upstairs and say hi to my mom, and maybe change into something a little more suited to crawling around in the dirt." Alyson started toward the stairs. "Help yourself to a snack. Whatever you can find."

Tucker followed Alyson up the stairs, as if reluctant to let her out of his sight for even a minute now that she was home. "Hi, Mom," Alyson said, poking her head through the door to the attic. "I just wanted to let you know I was home and that Mac and I are going to take Tucker for a run."

"Will she be staying for dinner?"

"No, I think she'll probably head home after we get back."

"How about trying out the diner in town you were telling me about tonight? I've been painting all day and I really don't feel much like cooking tonight."

"Sounds good. Now that I'm a licensed driver maybe we could go car shopping on the way."

"I think that can be arranged."

Alyson changed into an old pair of jeans and a paint-spattered Tommy Hilfiger T-shirt. She tied a red sweatshirt around her waist in case it was windy up on the bluff and dug out her oldest pair of Nike sneakers. After pulling her long straight hair into a sloppy ponytail, she headed back downstairs.

By the time she had rejoined Mac, Trevor had shown up carrying several flashlights. Alyson grabbed two shovels from the shed and they headed out. Tucker ran several yards ahead of them as they walked toward their destination, stopping occasionally to chase a bird or sniff a bush.

"Fall is definitely in the air." Mac wrapped her sweater tightly around her torso. "Did you get your fireplaces all cleared for use?"

"The guy will be here Tuesday. I can't wait. Tucker, wait up," Alyson called when she noticed the pup had wandered too far ahead. Tucker sat down in the middle of the path and waited for the others to catch up.

"He's trained really well. He should make a great guard dog once he matures a little," Trevor observed.

"Thank you for finding him for me. I'm enjoying him so much. It's a whole new experience to wake up to a dog staring you in the face."

"He stares you in the face?" Trevor asked.

"He sleeps next to the bed, and he's a really quiet sleeper, but once he wakes up and needs to go out, he'll put his head next to mine on the bed and wait for me to acknowledge him. I usually feel him breathing on me. But I don't mind. He gets so happy when I finally open my eyes. I can't tell you how great it is to wake up each morning to someone who's so thrilled to see me."

"My fish pretty much ignores me," Mac grumbled.

"Here we are," Trevor announced. "I'll go in first, in case there are any creepy crawlies. Once I get in, I'll check around, and if everything looks okay I'll give you a yell."

"Sounds good," the girls agreed.

Trevor got down on his stomach and squeezed through the small opening. After a couple of minutes they heard him yell for them to follow him.

"After you." Mac motioned to Alyson.

She took a deep breath and slithered through. The tiny entrance gave way to a huge room with two tunnels leading off into the dark cave.

The first thing Alyson noticed was the rest of the body they'd first stumbled across outside. "Who do you think it is?" Alyson looked toward the disheveled pile of bones.

"Ew," Mac said as she joined them. "It looks like he was torn apart."

The trio walked over to get a closer look. "What's that?" Alyson asked, pointing her flashlight at something shiny near the skeleton's chest.

Trevor bent down to get a better look. "Some sort of medallion." He gently lifted it from the skeleton, trying not to disturb the remains any more than they already were. "Looks old." He wiped his thumb across the dirt covering it to get a better look. "There's the image of a ship with the words *Santa Inez* stamped on the bottom. Wait. There's a date." He spit on the medallion and wiped it on the leg of his pants. "Eighteen twenty-six. Wow, that's old. And it looks like real gold."

"Who do you think he was?" Alyson queried.

"Maybe a pirate. Or a smuggler," Mac guessed. "If the rumors are true about Jedediah Cutter's illegal activities, this guy might have been one of the smugglers."

"But why was he just left here in the cave?" Alyson shivered. "Why didn't someone bury him?"

"Who knows?" Mac shrugged. "Maybe he tried to double-cross old Jedediah, so he killed him and left him here as a warning to anyone else who might have similar ideas."

"Okay," Trevor interrupted. "Now we're just making stuff up. Anything could have happened to this guy. We have no way of knowing, so let's just stick to what we do know."

"Which is?" Alyson asked.

"That we found a cave in the side of the cliff face, and it contains a dead guy who probably was a sailor and probably lived in the eighteen hundreds. There may or may not be something in here from Barkley's time. I suggest we look around, but for now stay in this large area. I don't think we should wander back into the tunnels until we're prepared, with better equipment."

The trio spent the next twenty minutes searching the floor and walls of the dark, damp cave. The main room was large enough to walk around in comfortably, but it was obvious that many of the arms that sectioned off from the main room were much smaller.

"What's that dripping sound?" Mac asked.

Everyone stopped to listen.

"It sounds like water dripping," Alyson observed. "I think it's coming from the tunnel to the left."

"We'll have to check it out another time," Trevor said. "I really don't feel prepared to go back into those tunnels now. Who knows what's back there?"

"I found something." Alyson held up a box about the size of a small toolbox. "Of course it's locked."

"It doesn't look particularly old or valuable, so I vote we break the lock," Mac said.

"Let's take it back to my house. I'm sure I can find some tools to open it with."

"What should we do with him?" Mac asked, gesturing toward the skeleton in the corner.

"Nothing for now," Trevor said. "He's most likely been here for over a hundred years. A few more days while we decide what to do won't hurt. Maybe we should bring the arm in here, though."

They crawled back through the opening, and then Trevor went back through with the arm. Once the site was camouflaged with nearby brush, they headed back toward the house.

"I think there are some tools out in the old carriage house." Alyson walked toward the crumbling building to the right of the main house and muscled open the large barn-style door. She walked toward the back, where a dilapidated toolbox was sitting atop an equally dilapidated metal counter. "There should be something in here." She rummaged through the box. "These should do." She held up a rusty pair of bolt cutters.

Trevor set the metal lockbox on the counter and, taking the bolt cutters from Alyson, squeezed down tightly until the lock popped. Trevor slowly opened the box, with Alyson and Mac looking on expectantly. Sitting right on the top was a large brass key.

"The key to the chest," Alyson whispered. She lifted it out and examined it.

Directly under the key was a small black leather journal. Mac took it out and opened it. "The pages are all written on, but this definitely isn't English."

Beneath the journal were a couple dozen coins. "It seems our smuggling theory is starting to get some teeth after all," Alyson said.

"What's under the coins?" Mac asked.

Trevor set them on the counter next to the box and took out the old hand-embroidered handkerchief, folded into quarters, which had been beneath it. Cradled inside was a photograph of a woman with dark hair and eyes leaning against the railing in front of the house. She was smiling in a way that seemed to indicate she shared a joke with the photographer. The house was in much better repair in the picture, so it must be fairly old.

"Is there any writing on the back?" Alyson asked hopefully.

Trevor turned the picture over. "No."

"Who do you think she is?" Mac wondered.

"Maybe it's Mary," Alyson ventured.

"We don't even know for sure this box belonged to Barkley," Trevor reminded them.

"Maybe there's a clue in the journal." Alyson opened the book to the front cover, but the owner's identity wasn't clearly evident. "If we can figure out what language this is, maybe we can have it translated. It might give us some clues."

The final object in the box was a legal document, folded in half. Alyson took it out and unfolded it. "I think we have our proof."

The document was a handwritten birth certificate, dated September 12, 1955. On the line indicating the name of the baby, it just said Jonathan, no last name. The line next to the father's name had been left blank, and the one next to the mother said Mary Swanson. Toward the bottom of the certificate was a place for the name of the attending physician. The name Stella Townsend had been printed neatly.

"Why do you think the father's name and the child's last name were omitted?" Mac asked.

"Maybe that was part of the deal Barkley made with Mary," Alyson suggested. "Or maybe in exchange for the monthly support check he was to have nothing to do with the child."

"Then why does he have the birth certificate?" Mac retorted. "If he truly wanted to wash his hands of the whole thing, why hang on to this rather incriminating piece of evidence?"

"I suppose we may never know," Alyson said.

Trevor began carefully placing the contents back into the box. "Let's go see if this key opens that big trunk in the attic. Maybe we'll find some answers there."

They walked quietly back to the house and up the stairs, each deep in their own thoughts.

"I thought I heard you guys come back," Alyson's mom greeted them as they filed in.

"I think we found the key to the trunk." Alyson held up the shiny brass object

"Where did you find it?" her mom asked.

They looked silently at one another, and Alyson decided it was time to come clean. Her mom had supported her to this point, and she deserved to know. Alyson filled her in on all the details she was missing. To her mom's credit, she didn't blink an eye when they told her about the cave and its current resident. Then the four of them went up to the attic and gathered around the trunk. Alyson slowly slipped the key into the heavy lock and gave it a hard clockwise turn. The lock popped open.

"Wow," Alyson said when she'd opened the trunk. "I had a lot of ideas about what might be in here, but never in my wildest dreams did I picture this."

She lifted out a long white christening gown. The entire trunk was filled with baby clothes, baby blankets, even baby toys.

"Do you think Mary brought Jonathan here to live after he was born?" she whispered.

"Looks like." Her mother lifted out a well-preserved brown teddy bear with a bright red ribbon around its neck.

"But if Barkley acknowledged his son, why isn't the birth certificate fully filled out, and why doesn't anyone know about Jonathan?" Mac wondered.

"We know Mary moved up to Washington about a year after Jonathan was born. Maybe they just agreed to a trial run, and the birth certificate would be completed and Jonathan acknowledged if things worked out," Trevor guessed.

"Now who's creating stories to match the evidence?" Alyson teased.

"Maybe the Stella Townsend is still around," Mac speculated. "If we could find her, she could probably fill in the missing pieces to the puzzle."

"We could check the telephone directory. Or ask around in town if that doesn't pan out," Mac suggested.

They carefully folded and replaced the contents from the trunk, then filed downstairs in search of a phone book.

"There isn't a listing for a Townsend." Alyson closed the book in frustration.

"Maybe someone in town remembers her and knows what happened to her," Mac said.

"Ben." Alyson opened the book, searched for the *W*s, and started dialing. "Mr. Wilson," Alyson began when he answered, "this is Alyson Prescott. I came by with my friend Trevor the other day." She stopped to listen. "Yes, it was fun. I have another question for you, if you have a moment." She paused. "I'm sure you are. Hey, listen, do you remember someone from about the time we were talking with you about named Stella Townsend?" Alyson wrapped the phone cord around her finger as she listened. "You don't say. Do you know where we might find her now?" Alyson picked up the message pad by the phone and started to write. "Thank you. You've been very helpful." She stared at the clock over the kitchen sink. "Yes, we'll have to do that. . . . Yes, I promise. . . . Okay, good-bye now."

Alyson hung up the phone and turned toward the others. "It seems Stella Townsend was a midwife. Unfortunately, she moved out of town quite a few years back, and Ben isn't sure where she went. He did say that Stella has a daughter who still lives in town. Her name is Ashley Kent." Alyson opened the phone book to the *K*s. "There's only one Kent listed, so that must be her. I'm not sure this is a phone call type of conversation, though. Maybe we should wait until tomorrow to see if we can talk to her in person."

"We have a half day at school tomorrow," Mac reminded her. "Should give us plenty of time to try to talk to her before the game."

"Sounds like a plan."

Mac looked at her watch. "I'd better get going. My mom's not much of a cook, but she likes us there to eat what she makes."

Alyson saw Trevor and Mac off, then returned to the house to see if her mom was ready to go into town for dinner.

After several hours and four test-drives, Alyson decided on a four-door Jeep Wrangler. The four-wheel-drive vehicle had enough room for all of her new friends and Tucker in the back. It was white with a soft top, so she could go topless in the summer. Thanks to her very generous mom, she also had a top-of-the-line stereo installed, as well as a GPS navigation system.

After a celebratory dinner with her mom, Alyson called her new friends to tell them about the newest addition to her family as soon as they got home.

"Wow, that's great," Mac congratulated her. "My car is a hand-me-down from my hippie grandmother. I love my car for its sentimental value, but it's kind of small and tends to be temperamental."

"Your car has character," Alyson commented. "Don't get me wrong, I love my new car, but if I had the chance to own a hand-me-down from a grandmother I'd take it."

"Is your grandmother still alive?" Mac asked.

Alyson hesitated. While her grandmother was alive, she believed that *Alyson* was dead.

"She's alive, but we aren't close," Alyson compromised.

"That's too bad. Is there any family you are close to? Other than your mother?"

"No. Not really. Did you hear from Eli?" Alyson decided it was best to change the subject.

"I did. He talked to his brother and he's agreed to do a little snooping for us tomorrow. He said he'll introduce us to him after the game."

"That's great. I'm getting really anxious to wrap up this mystery. For one thing, even with Tucker and the new locks the guys installed, I don't feel entirely safe with whoever broke in the other day still out there."

"Maybe you guys should get a security system. Something high-tech, like the rich people have. You're awful far off the beaten path. If something happened you wouldn't even have any neighbors to call on."

"Yeah, maybe. I'll talk to my mom about it. I guess I should go finish my homework so I can get to bed at a decent time. Tomorrow's going to be a long day."

Chapter 12

The group met in the parking lot next to Alyson's new Jeep after school the next day. Tonight was the big game, so they only had a limited amount of time for what they needed to do.

"Eli and I need to be back on campus by four o'clock." Trevor calculated. "That gives us about four hours to track down Stella Townsend."

"I have both a phone number and an address for Ashley Kent," Alyson reminded them. "Should we try going to her house or should we call first?"

"I say we call." Mac leaned against the shiny white SUV. "We might go all the way over there only to find out she isn't home. A lot of people are probably at work at this time of day."

Alyson pulled out her cell phone. "What should I say if she's there? Just blurting out that we're looking for her mother might seem odd."

"Just tell her we're doing papers for history, interviewing longtime residents," Trevor suggested. "It worked okay with Ben. Then we can just sort of ease into the topic of her mom once we get her talking."

Alyson dialed the number on the slip of paper in her hand. "May I speak to Ashley Kent?" she asked whoever answered the phone on the other end. "I see. Can you tell me when she might be home?" Alyson waited for the reply. "And where exactly does she work? Okay, thanks. I'll do that."

Alyson hung up the phone and slipped it back into her purse. "I think one of her kids answered. He told me she would be at work until six o'clock, at the local library."

"That's not far from here," Mac said. "Let's go see if she has time to talk to us right now."

They climbed into the Jeep and drove the two short blocks to the county library. "Do you think we should all go in?" Eli asked. "It might be overwhelming to have all four of us descend on her at once."

Alyson agreed. "Maybe Trevor and Mac should go in. They've lived here a lot longer than Eli and I have and could probably present a much more believable story. I mean, if we really were doing a paper, we'd already know something about the town, and Eli and I really don't."

"That's a good idea." Mac nodded. "Come on, pretty boy, let's go work some magic."

"Don't call me that," Trevor complained as he got out of the passenger seat and followed Mac up the walkway to the front of the building.

"Those two act more like siblings than friends," Eli observed.

"I noticed that the first day I met them. Mac told me they've been friends since they were in diapers. I guess that sort of makes them like siblings, although Mac is always complaining that she doesn't get along with her real brother and sisters. Do you get along with your brother?" Alyson asked.

"Most times I do. He's older than me, but we've always been close. I take it you don't have siblings?"

"No, it's just me," Alyson confirmed.

"It must be lonely to be an only child."

Alyson shrugged. "Sometimes. But my mom and I are close, and I've always had good friends. So, are you starting in today's game?"

Alyson and Eli talked about football while they waited. While the conversation was interesting, it seemed like Mac and Trevor had been gone forever. Alyson looked at her watch. Twenty minutes had passed and they still hadn't come out of the library.

"Well, at least she didn't kick them out immediately," Eli said, when Alyson commented on how long they'd been gone.

"True. But I really hate all this waiting around. I wish they'd hurry."

"Here they come," Eli announced.

Trevor and Mac got back into the Jeep and Alyson started the engine.

"Stella Townsend lives in a small town that's about thirty miles down the coast," Mac began. "Ashley was kind enough to call her mom, who agreed to see us this afternoon."

"Do we have time?" Alyson asked. "It's already almost one, and it will take a good forty minutes to drive there on the coast road. And that's if there's no traffic."

"It might be cutting it close on a Friday afternoon," Trevor acknowledged. "Coach will have a coronary if we're late. Maybe you two should go without us. The game doesn't actually start until six, so you should have plenty of time."

Alyson looked at Mac.

"Yeah, that's probably a good idea," Mac agreed.

Alyson headed south down the coast highway. "This sure is a pretty drive," she said, noting the crashing waves and rocky cliffs to their right. "The water near Cutter's Cove doesn't seem quite this rough."

"That's because the town was built on an inlet," Mac explained. "There's a natural wave break a few miles out that protects the cove."

"You know, I've lived in Cutter's Cove a month and I haven't even been down to the beach."

"There's a great beach at the end of Miller's Road," Mac told her. "Everyone around here goes there because it's got a huge strip of sand and the water is usually nice and calm. We should try to go before the weather gets too cold. It's really fun to have a huge bonfire and roast marshmallows. And we could make s'mores. I love the way the marshmallows smoosh out the sides of the graham crackers."

"Sounds like fun." Alyson smiled at Mac's childlike enthusiasm. "Maybe next weekend?"

"There'll be a game on Saturday, but maybe Sunday. Do you surf?"

"I've never tried, but I'd like to. It seems like the water would be too cold, though."

"Most surfers wear wet suits this far north. You should try it," Mac encouraged. "It's a real rush."

The drive took nearly an hour with Friday-afternoon traffic, but finally they pulled up in front of a neat Cape Cod–style house. Stella must have a green thumb; the entire property boasted neatly groomed landscaping.

"Wow, those flowers along the front of the porch are gorgeous," Mac observed.

"So, do we stick to our school-paper approach or do we get right to the point?" Alyson asked as they sat outside the house. "Sooner or later we're going to have to come right out and ask her if Jonathan was Barkley's son."

"Maybe we should get right to the point, but in a roundabout way. We could start off telling her that your mom bought the house and ease into the whole heir thing from there. Did you bring the birth certificate?"

"It's in my purse."

Mac took a deep breath for courage. "Okay, let's do this."

Alyson and Mac walked up the four steps to the front door. Alyson rang the doorbell. The few seconds it took for someone to answer seemed like an eternity.

"You must be the kids from Cutter's Cove." A friendly-looking older woman wearing a sundress opened the door. "Come on in. I've made lemonade."

The interior of the house was as neat and cheerily decorated as the front yard. "We'll sit outside." The woman indicated they should take seats at the bright yellow picnic table that sat in the center of a large brick patio.

"You have a beautiful home," Alyson said. "And your garden is stunning."

"Thank you. I enjoy it. Gardening is a hobby of mine." The woman poured three glasses of freshly squeezed lemonade and passed them around. "So, should we get right to the point?" she asked.

Alyson hesitated. She'd been all ready to go into her hastily prepared speech, but she hadn't been expecting the woman's forthrightness.

"You're here about Jonathan, aren't you?" she asked when Alyson didn't say anything.

Both girls looked across the table, their mouths hanging open.

"I knew the moment Ashley called that was the real reason for this visit," the woman informed them.

"Yes," Alyson croaked. "But how did you know?"

"I know a lot of things," the feisty woman replied. "You don't get to be eighty-two years old without knowing a thing or two."

"I want you to know we have only the best of intentions," Alyson interjected quickly. We're not trying to damage anyone's reputation or betray anyone's secrets; it's just that after we started sorting through all the stuff in the attic, we realized there might be a legitimate heir. We simply wanted to find him and return his stuff to him."

"And that led you to Jonathan."

"Yes, ma'am." Alyson looked toward Mac, who seemed quite shocked still and hadn't said a word. "We have reason to believe that Jonathan's son, Caleb, is the rightful heir to whatever is left of the Cutter fortune. Unfortunately, we don't have any absolute proof. We found the birth certificate, but there isn't any father's name on it. Without a witness or some other documentation, it might not stand up in court if someone challenged his right to his inheritance."

Stella stood up from the table and walked over to pick a spent bud from the rosebush near the back door. Returning to the table, she looked Alyson in the eye and spoke again. "When Ashley called I knew what you were after. I actually wasn't sure what I was going to do before you girls showed up. I made a promise over fifty years ago that I've kept ever since. However," she sat back down in her chair, "everyone I made that promise to is dead. I see no reason to keep quiet any longer. Especially if it will help you to make sure Barkley's grandson gets what he deserves."

"So Jonathan really was Barkley's son," Alyson whispered.

"Indeed he was," Stella declared. "And I have the original copy of the birth certificate, which lists both parents' names, to prove it."

"You mean the one we found isn't the only copy?"

"You have to understand," Stella started to explain, "Mary was a little slip of a girl when she met Barkley. She fell madly in love with him and he, in his own way, loved her too. When she got pregnant Barkley wanted Mary to take the baby and start a new life somewhere else. He knew Jonathan would never have a normal life with him. His reputation as an eccentric was already firmly established, and most of the townsfolk thought he'd killed his stepmother. A normal life in Cutter's Cove for anyone with the name Cutter was never going to happen."

Stella took a sip of her lemonade. "Besides, Barkley had been a bastard son himself, and he associated illegitimacy with pain. His entire life his stepmom, as well as many of the town's citizens, had ostracized and abused him. He knew he couldn't be the father Jonathan deserved, so he arranged for an old friend of his to marry Mary and adopt the boy."

Stella paused for breath. "Thing was, Mary loved Barkley and would have nothing to do with the idea. Finally, after months of bargaining, the two struck a deal. Mary would have the baby, but she wouldn't leave town. She had to promise, however, never to tell anyone Barkley was the father. Mary came to me and we struck a deal; in exchange for quite a lot of money, I would deliver the baby without ever revealing the true paternity of the child. The birth certificate you found was a copy of the original."

Stella took another sip of her drink. "After Jonathan was born Mary somehow convinced Barkley to let them move in with him. No one in town knew about it, mostly because no one in town ever went out to the estate except to deliver supplies, and by that time no one really expected to catch a glimpse of the estate's occupant. I know Mary loved Barkley with all her heart, but she finally realized after a year of living with a total recluse that was no way to bring up a child. Finally, she agreed to Barkley's original offer and moved north to marry the man he picked out for her. I believe it was a marriage in name only. I really only know this much because Mary came to me to get a second copy of the birth certificate. She filled in her new husband's name as the father, although I don't know if she ever filed it anywhere."

Alyson wiped a tear from her cheek. "Why didn't Barkley simply move with Mary and his son? Somewhere new, where no one knew them?"

"I've often wondered that myself. He seemed to care for Mary and the boy, but I think it was too late. For some reason we may never know, he made that home of his into a prison. I don't think he could get past his own neurosis. He seemed totally incapable of being a part of normal society by that point."

Mac spoke for the first time. "You said you have a signed copy of the birth certificate. When did he sign it?"

"After Mary left, he called and had me come out to the house so he could sign it. He made me promise I would keep it secret until after he died."

"So why didn't you bring forth the evidence of Jonathan's birth when Barkley died?" Alyson asked.

"I didn't know until recently that Jonathan's son even existed. I knew Barkley had died, but I didn't realize Jonathan had come back to Cutter's Cove, or that he'd married and had a child. I moved away a long time ago and didn't keep up with local news. And Jonathan's last name was Wellington. I had no way of knowing he was Barkley's son."

"So how did you realize who he was, and find out about Caleb?" Alyson asked.

"Ben Wilson called me a few days ago to tell me about the questions some kids had been asking. He knew I'd delivered Mary's baby but not the rest of the story. I've been trying to figure out what to do since he called. Then, when Ashley called this afternoon, I decided to meet you myself to see what you were up to. If your intentions were pure, I decided to tell you the whole story. If they hadn't been I would have made up a lie."

"Wow," Mac breathed, leaning back in her chair. "I thought I'd be happy to have this mystery solved, and I *am* happy we can help Caleb get what's coming to him, but I feel so sad. Totally drained. I really wasn't prepared for that."

They talked with Stella for another half hour or so, then decided they'd better head back to Cutter's Cove. Stella had given them the signed copy of the birth certificate, and they'd promised to get it to Caleb as soon as possible.

"So when should we talk to Caleb?" Mac asked on the ride back.

Alyson glanced at her watch. "It's getting late. We'll probably miss the start of the game as it is."

"He's probably already there," Mac added. "Everyone in Cutter's Cove goes to the first home game of the season."

"I guess we can try to talk to him tomorrow, after the breakfast and the parade."

"I think that would be best," Mac agreed.

The ride back to Cutter's Cove was a silent one, each girl consumed with her own thoughts.

By the time Alyson and Mac got to the game the players were already being announced. They found seats near the middle of the bleachers, where they had a good view of the entire field. Alyson stood up to scan the bleachers around them. "My mom was going to meet us here. I'm never going to find her in this crowd."

Mac turned in her seat to help her look. "I think that's her, over by the fence behind the goalpost. It looks like she brought Tucker with her."

Alyson looked where Mac was pointing and saw her mom sitting with Tucker on the grass at the far end of the field, talking to a man Alyson had never seen before.

"Who's she talking to?" Alyson asked.

"I think that's Mr. Sanders. He owns an art gallery on Main Street. His son Jeff plays defense for the team. Oh, they're lining up for the kickoff. Go Pirates! Kick some Sunnyside ass!"

The crowd all around them began to roar as the ball was kicked high into the air. A tall blond boy in a Pirates uniform caught the ball and ran down the field.

"Show 'em what you've got, Joel." Mac was on her feet now. "Come on; run, baby, run!"

Mac finally sat down once the runner was forced out of bounds. "Did you see that return? Had to be a fifty-yard play. We are *so* going to take state this year."

Mac's enthusiasm was infectious and Alyson soon found herself cheering as loudly as anyone. It might seem odd that Alyson had made it to the ripe old age of sixteen without ever having been to a football game. Her dad had never been interested in sports, and she didn't have any brothers to educate her. Most of her male friends had been more interested in partying than joining athletic teams, and the few glimpses of sporting events she'd come across from time to time on television screens in homes other than her own had bored her. This, however, was fun.

"There's Trevor." Alyson pointed to the offensive team lining up on the field. "And Eli's to his left. Number 32."

"Go Pirates!" Mac was on her feet again.

By the end of the night the Pirates had won, 28–7, and Alyson was completely hoarse from yelling.

"Look at that ho, Madison Richards," Mac complained as the players congratulated one another after the final buzzer. "She's hanging all over Eli like she owns him."

Alyson looked toward the field. A blonde cheerleader had her arms around Eli's neck.

"Oh my God. Is she kissing him?" Mac shouted. "What a total skank."

"Eli made three touchdowns tonight," Alyson reminded her friend. "He's on everyone's radar now. Do I detect a little jealousy there?"

"No," Mac denied. "No jealousy. I just don't want to see Eli get hurt. He's my friend, and Madison Richards is a user."

"I'm going to go say hi to my mom before we head over to the bonfire." Alyson changed the subject. "I'll meet you outside the locker room. I'm sure it will be a while before Trevor and Eli make it out of there."

Alyson wended her way through the crowd in search of her mother. Mac was correct; everyone in town had indeed shown up for the game. It was going to take a real effort to make it through the droves of fans still on the field.

"Hi, Mom," Alyson said when she finally made her way to the goalpost. She knelt down to pet an ecstatic Tucker. "I saw you from the bleachers, but it looked like you had company so I didn't come over." Alyson took a peek at the good-looking man who was still standing beside her mother.

"This is Blake Sanders," Alyson's mom introduced them. "He owns an art gallery downtown." She turned to Blake. "This is my daughter, Alyson."

"It's good to meet you." Blake smiled. "Your mother has just been telling me about some of the paintings she's working on. I'd love to see them sometime."

"She's great." Alyson stood up from her position by the dog. "I think you'll be impressed."

"Blake has asked me to join him for coffee. Do you think you could take Tucker with you to the bonfire?"

"Sure, Mom." Alyson shook off her melancholy and smiled. "I'll walk over to the car with you and get his travel crate."

Alyson took the leash from her mom and followed her out to the parking lot. After transferring the crate to the back of her Jeep, she kissed her mom on the cheek and went in search of her friends.

The bonfire was one of the most outrageous events Alyson had ever attended. Most of the participants were students of Seacliff High. Everyone was dancing around, singing and cheering. In the center of all the commotion was a huge bonfire that lit the entire area. At first Alyson was concerned that bringing Tucker to such a crowded place might not have been such a good idea, but he just sat at her feet and watched the festivities around him.

"Hey, guys." Eli walked toward them with Madison clinging to his arm.

"Great game!" Mac hugged Eli awkwardly. "You totally rocked. That one reception in the third quarter . . . I mean, it was totally awesome."

"So, Eli," Trevor joined in, "are we on for that thing tomorrow?"

"Thing?"

Trevor looked pointedly at Eli.

"Oh, that thing. Yeah, sure. We'll meet up at the breakfast."

"What thing?" Madison asked.

"Oh, it's just a guy thing," Eli said evasively. "Listen, Madison, why don't you go see if you can find us some drinks."

"Sure. Okay," Madison said doubtfully. "I'll be right back."

"What's with the groupie?" Alyson asked as the cheerleader walked away.

"She just sort of attached herself to me after the game and I haven't been able to shake her."

"Want me to get rid of her?" Mac volunteered a little too cheerfully.

"That's okay," Eli said. "She's not really my type, but being seen with her is probably good for my rep. I am the new guy, you know. I guess I shouldn't look a gift horse in the mouth."

"She does sort of look like a horse," Mac muttered under her breath.

"I want to introduce you to my brother. Hey, Devon!" Eli called over a tall guy with blond hair who had been talking to one of the cheerleaders. "These are my friends, Alyson, Mac, and Trevor."

"Glad to meet you all."

Devon was tall, blond, and gorgeous. Not at all what Alyson had been expecting. She wasn't sure why, but when Eli had described his brother's advanced level of computer literacy she'd been expecting a nerd. Devon was anything but. Mac gently elbowed her, and Alyson realized her mouth was hanging wide open. She hoped she wasn't drooling.

"Devon did a little snooping around, as I promised he would, and has some interesting news to share," Eli informed the group.

"Whatcha got?" Alyson asked.

"I've had a part-time job at the police station since we moved to Cutter's Cove at the beginning of the summer, entering old records into the new computer system. Eli told me about the project you are working on and asked me to see if I could get a look at Jonathan Wellington's suicide report. I did as he asked and stumbled across something I found interesting. There were two sets of fingerprints on the suicide note. One belonged to Caleb's mother, who was the one who found the note in the first place, and the other couldn't be identified. The interesting thing is that Jonathan's fingerprints weren't found on the note at all."

"So he couldn't have written it," Alyson realized.

"Probably not, unless he was wearing gloves when he wrote the note, but why would someone who was about to kill himself do that?"

"So why wasn't the fingerprint angle looked into further at the time of his death?" Alyson wondered.

"I don't know. There were conflicting reports, so it sort of depends on who you talk to."

"So the answer to who killed Jonathan could lie in figuring out who the second set of fingerprints belongs to. Don't the police have basically everyone's fingerprints on file?"

"Unfortunately, no."

"So now what?" Alyson asked.

"I have a few ideas, but maybe we should take this conversation somewhere else," Devon suggested.

"We could go get something to eat," Trevor suggested.

"Sounds good to me," Eli answered. "How about Pirates Pizza?"

"I left my car in the parking lot near the gym," Trevor informed them. "I rode over to the bonfire with a friend."

"I'll give you a ride to your car," Alyson offered.

"We'll meet you at the restaurant," Alyson said to Devon and Eli.

Alyson, Mac, and Trevor headed to Alyson's car. They piled in and pulled into the parking lot in front of the gym a few minutes later. Alyson noticed that the light was on inside. "Who do you think is in the gym?"

Mac frowned. "I'm not sure. I know there were people here decorating for the dance earlier, but I thought they'd left."

"Let's check it out," Alyson suggested. "It'd be a shame if someone was vandalizing the place."

Alyson clipped the leash on Tucker and let him out of the cargo area of the Jeep. The trio walked across the pavement toward the front door.

"That's Caleb Wellington over there," Trevor leaned close and whispered as they stood in the entry. "He's the dark-haired boy with the Pirates sweatshirt working on the sound system. He always does the decorations for these things."

"Should we tell him what we know?" Mac asked.

"I'd wait," Alyson said.

"He has no idea his life's about to change forever," Trevor observed.

"That's usually the way it happens." Alyson reached down to scratch Tucker behind his right ear. "One moment you're living a perfectly normal life and the next everything's changed." Alyson bit her lip. "I mean, this is definitely going to be one of those life-defining moments in Caleb's life. The kind that slams into you and leaves you gasping for air. But it's a good thing, right? He'll be happy? Better off?" Alyson didn't sound sure at all.

"Of course he will," Mac assured her friend. "This is going to be great for him. He'll have so many options open to him that he might not have otherwise had." Mac wove her arm through Alyson's in a show of camaraderie "I heard his mom has had to struggle since his dad died. She's been working two jobs. Now she won't have to work at all. It'll be great."

"I guess." Alyson still sounded unsure.

"Who's that guy over by the bandstand?" Alyson whispered. "Is he a teacher or something?"

"Never seen him before," Mac answered. "It looks like he's spying on Caleb."

Alyson watched as Caleb continued to test the sound system. He appeared to be alone, his back toward the man watching him. Alyson couldn't help but wonder if he even knew he was there. Tucker began to growl. Alyson looked from Tucker to Caleb and then back toward the man, who hadn't as of yet noticed him.

"Oh my God!" Alyson handed Tucker's leash to Mac and took off at a run.

"What's going on?" Caleb asked as Alyson threw herself in front of him. "Who are you?"

"You're ruining everything!" the man screamed as he ran across the room, waving a gun around. "I should have burned that pile of timber down when I had the chance."

"Shooting us won't do you any good," Alyson insisted once she realized the man was Steven Laslow. During her research, she'd come across a recent photo of the man, although in it he'd been dressed in a three-piece suit. She hadn't recognized him at first; he looked a lot different dressed down as he was tonight.

"Too many people know you're embezzling from the trust," Alyson added. "It's over."

"It's not over until I say it is." The hand holding the gun was shaking badly. "I deserve it. I spent my entire life building that fortune. He didn't do anything." He waved the gun toward Caleb."

The man was still rambling, the gun pointed at Caleb, then abruptly pulled the trigger. At the same instant, Tucker, who had pulled free of Mac's grasp, jumped on him, viciously biting his arm. The motion caused the bullet to fly harmlessly over Caleb's head. Trevor, who had made his way across the room, attempted to pull the dog off, but he wasn't letting go.

"Tucker, come," Alyson screamed as soon as she could catch her breath.

The dog looked up and immediately came over to Alyson and sat obediently in front of her, though he continued to growl as he stared at the man on the ground. Trevor wrestled him into a standing position.

"Guess we'd better call the cops."

Chapter 13

"I feel like I've been run over by a truck." Alyson groaned, rubbing the back of her neck with her fingertips.

"It's no wonder. We had quite a night. Did you ever in your wildest dreams imagine it would end like this?" Mac took a huge bite of her pancake. "I pictured us meeting with Caleb and his mom this afternoon. Maybe having tea. Sharing with them the wonderful news that they were now the richest people in Cutter's Cove. There would be tears of joy. Hugs and kisses. Maybe even an invite to some future celebratory event. But this." Mac paused to swallow, "This I never, ever imagined."

"The whole thing is pretty mind boggling," Trevor agreed. "I hope Caleb's okay. He looked pretty shaken up last night."

"Well, sure," Eli observed, "Someone tried to kill him."

"No, it was more than that," Trevor countered. "I was watching his face while we told him the story about Barkley and how his dad fit in. He looked kind of freaked."

"Well, it's some story," Alyson said. "We were pretty freaked when we first heard it and we're not even biologically connected. Besides, learning that your father was probably murdered has to have a profound effect on someone."

"By the way," Eli changed the subject, "I invited Devon to go to the dance with us. I hope that's okay. Even though he hasn't actually started classes yet, he's a Seacliff student for the next few months."

"Sure, that'd be great." Alyson smiled. "Speaking of the dance—" She was interrupted by Madison's arrival.

"It's time to go over to the staging area," she cooed to Eli, leaning up against him as she spoke.

Trevor looked at his watch. "We've got to go. The football team is riding on one of the floats. We'll see you guys tonight."

"Tonight?" Madison asked Eli as he stood to follow Trevor.

"We're all going to the dance together."

"I could use a ride." Madison snuggled closer.

"Sorry, we're all full up," Eli answered.

"Oh." Madison pouted. "I guess we can just meet up at the dance, then."

"Maybe," Eli said vaguely.

"I can't believe the way Madison hangs all over Eli," Mac complained as they walked away. "She's just like Chelsea."

"I know I've asked you this before," Alyson said tentatively, "but I have to say I'm sensing something a little more than a friend looking out for a friend going on here. I'm sensing jealousy."

"There might be a little jealousy," Mac reluctantly acknowledged. "I don't know. I've really only known Eli a little over a week."

"Yeah, but it's been some week," Alyson reasoned.

Mac pushed her half-eaten plate of pancakes away. "I certainly don't have any reason to feel Eli should have any type of commitment to me. It just bugs me that he lets Madison hang all over him."

"If you like him you should tell him. Make the first move. Ask him out."

"Oh, I couldn't do that." Mac blushed.

"Why not? Madison certainly isn't being shy about her feelings for him. Why should you? If you want him, fight for him. If you don't," Alyson placed her hand over Mac's on the table, "she may end up with him by default."

"How am I supposed to compete with someone like Madison? She's pretty and popular and a cheerleader to boot." Mac looked down at herself. "I'm just a spaz. Look at me. I have a cow on my shirt. How dorky is that?"

Mac had a point, Alyson realized. A T-shirt with a got milk? ad and bright pink sweatpants certainly made a statement, though she wasn't sure it was the one Mac was after. "I have an idea. Why don't we skip the parade and have a total spa day? I have tons of nice things you could wear to the dance, including several options in the blue and gray category. We could do your hair, maybe add a little makeup."

"I don't know . . ." Mac hesitated.

"Come on, what do you have to lose? We'll have Eli drooling over you."

Mac thought about it for a minute. "I'm in. Let's show Madison Fancy-pants she's not the only fish in the sea."

"That's the spirit."

The rest of the day was spent waxing, plucking, washing, and polishing every part of Mac's body.

"I had no idea," Mac commented as Alyson painted her toenails, "that so much work went into this. I have a new respect for Chelsea. But not for Madison. The slut," she added under her breath.

"My mom said she'd do your hair. She's the best. Why don't you hop in the shower and wash it real good, then we'll dry and style it."

Alyson went through her closet and picked out a selection of dresses for Mac to choose from. She laid everything across her bed, then went to find her mother to tell her they were ready for her.

"You have really beautiful hair," Alyson's mom complimented as Mac sat on a stool in front of her. "I don't think I've ever seen it down."

"I mostly wear pigtails and braids."

"It's so thick. And it's got a beautiful natural wave. I think we should just dry it and add a little gel to encourage the hair to curl. Then maybe we could just pull up the sides and let the back hang loose. I have a couple of mother-of-pearl combs that would be perfect to hold the hair back from your face," Sarah Prescott added.

"Whatever you think." Mac fidgeted on the stool.

Alyson's mom added some curling gel to Mac's thick hair, then dried it with a diffuser. She used the curling iron to smooth and define the curls, then pulled her hair up on the sides. Her long red hair cascaded down her back in perfect ringlets.

"Now for a little makeup," Alyson declared when her mom was finished.

"Are you sure?" Mac asked. "I don't usually wear makeup. I still want to look like me. A vastly improved me, but still me."

Alyson opened her makeup case and started to sort through its contents. "I'll keep it light. You'll hardly even know it's there. It will just make you look more . . ." she searched for the right word, "finished."

Alyson applied just the right makeup in just the right shades to bring out Mac's natural features without making her look overdone.

"You're really good at this," Mac commented as she watched her face transform layer by layer. "Where'd you ever learn to apply makeup like this?"

"I was a model for a while," Alyson responded without thinking.

"In Minnesota?"

"Yeah, Minnesota." Alyson crossed her fingers on her left hand as she lightly brushed blusher across Mac's cheekbone with her right. "Just for a local catalogue, but the makeup artist who worked the shoot taught me how to do this."

"Wow, a model." Mac was impressed "Was it fun? Do you still have the pictures?"

"Yeah, it was fun, and no, I don't have the pictures." The shoot had taken place in New York, and the background scenes were sure to give that away. The lies seemed to be getting harder, not easier. Alyson was letting her guard down. She'd have to do a better job of keeping her past firmly behind her.

"All done," she said several minutes later. "Take a look."

"Wow." Mac sounded awed when she turned to look in the mirror. "Is that me?"

"One hundred percent Makenzie Reynolds. Well, almost."

"I look so different. Do you think Eli will like it?"

"He'll love it. All the guys will. You'll have to fight them off. Now for the clothes. I've laid some stuff out on the bed. Wear whatever you want."

The girls migrated from the bathroom into the bedroom. Mac walked over to the bed and picked up a cashmere sweater. "Where did you get all this stuff?"

"They let me keep the clothes I modeled," Alyson lied.

"But these are big-time designer brands. I thought you said you modeled for a local catalogue?"

"I did, but it was an outlet store. Designer brands at bargain prices." *I'm going to hell for sure with all these lies.*

Alyson held up a short pleated skirt. "This is cute. It's not too long, not too short, not too fancy, yet not too casual. You could wear it with that dark blue silk tank and that light blue cardigan. I think I have the perfect gray suede boots to go with it."

"Do you think it will fit?" Mac held the skirt up to herself in the full-length mirror.

"Try it on and see. I'll look for the boots."

Mac tried on the outfit while Alyson rummaged through her closet for the boots, trying not to attract Mac's attention. The last thing she wanted her to see was an entire closet full of designer clothes.

"You look great," Alyson said, joining her in front of the mirror with the boots in her hand.

"Think so?" Mac turned from side to side "I don't want to look slutty, and this skirt is a little short."

"Trust me, you look beautiful. Eli's going to lose his cookies. Well, not literally."

"What are you going to wear?" Mac asked.

Alyson walked over to the bed to survey her options. "How about the blue denim skirt with the gray silk tank? I have a long navy sweater around here somewhere, and a pair of denim platform heels."

The pair finished dressing just as Devon pulled up out front. Mac grabbed Alyson's arm as she headed toward the stairs. "I don't know if I can do this. I feel like a fake."

"The secret to pulling off a new image is to *be* the image. You look great, really great. Hold your head high and act like you dress like this every day. Confidence is the key. One of the reasons I chose you to sit with that first day was because you looked like someone with a lot of self-confidence; someone who wasn't concerned about what other people thought."

"Really?"

"Really. Now let's go. We don't want to keep everyone waiting."

Devon had obviously chosen to pick them up last. He was the one driving because he had an Expedition that sat eight. Trevor was already seated in the third row, with Chelsea glued to his side, and Eli sat in front, next to Devon.

"Wow," Alyson heard Trevor exclaim from the backseat. "You guys look great." Looking directly at Mac, he added, "Who knew you'd clean up so well?"

"Shut up, Trevor," Mac barked as she tried to climb into the tall vehicle without exposing anything that ought not be exposed.

"Trade with me, Eli," Alyson said, crossing her fingers as she opened the front door. "I still feel a little dizzy from last night and I think I'll do better in the front."

"Are you okay?" Eli asked, concerned, as he vacated the front seat, helped Alyson in, and then climbed into the back."

"I'm fine. Just a little off."

Alyson pulled down her visor, even though the sun was already down, so she could watch the passengers in the backseat through the vanity mirror. Eli was staring at Mac, although he tried to appear as if he wasn't. He started to look away, but his gaze kept finding its way back.

"That whole thing last night was just the worst," Chelsea piped up from the third-row seat. "Once the cops showed up at the school it totally ruined the bonfire, and it's all anyone could talk about all day today at the parade. I for one hope it's not the topic of conversation at the dance. The kickoff to football dance is supposed to be all about the team and the cheerleaders. We don't need some lunatic with a gun clouding our focus."

Alyson looked in the mirror at Chelsea. A hooker would be embarrassed in the dress she had on. Besides, it was red, not blue or gray. "Don't worry; I'm sure your dress is the only thing anyone will be talking about at the dance."

Alyson heard Devon snicker beside her.

"You think so?" Chelsea's breasts threatened to spill out of her low-cut bodice as she spoke. "It's so sweet of you to say so. I had to try on like fifty dresses before I found one that fit this well."

The gym had been transformed into a pirate ship, minus the water, of course. Someone had gone to a lot of work to design props that made it appear that there were masts and rigging supporting giant sails that sported large crossbones. Oak barrels, joined together by heavy sailor's rope, had been set around the room. There were several students dressed as pirates to add to the setting.

"This is great," Alyson said as she walked in the door. "Someone did a lot of work."

"Personally, I think it's rather crass and predictable," Chelsea said from behind her. "I voted for the moonlight-in-paradise theme, but, once again, the pirate theme got picked."

"What does moonlight in paradise have to do with either football or our mascot?" Mac asked sharply.

"Nothing, I guess. It's just so much more romantic."

The group had barely filed into the gym when Madison was at Eli's side. "Do you want to dance? I've been waiting for you."

He took Mac by the arm. "I've already promised this dance to Mac. Maybe later," he said vaguely.

"Come on." Chelsea pulled Trevor toward the dance floor. "I need to get out there and be seen. The cheerleaders should make a point to be seen in order to show our support," she clarified, as if even she realized how lame she sounded.

Devon and Alyson wandered over to find a table. "It looks like Eli and Mac are having fun," Alyson commented.

"I think Eli kind of likes her. He's just too shy to ask her out."

"Really?" Alyson drawled. "He doesn't seem all that shy around Madison."

"Madison's been making all the moves. With her, Eli doesn't have to initiate anything. I think he finds that easier than asking someone out."

"So how about you? You shy?" Alyson asked.

"Hardly," Devon responded.

"You don't have to sit here with me all night just because you gave me a ride. If you have a girl you've been dying to get your arms around, now's your chance."

"Actually," Devon answered, "there *is* a girl I've been dying to get my arms around. Come on, let's dance." He pulled her onto the dance floor.

Alyson and Devon danced for an hour straight before she finally insisted that she really was getting dizzy and might pass out if she didn't take a break.

"I'll get us some punch," he offered. "Go find a table."

Alyson looked around the room and saw the others still dancing, so she took an empty table and sat down, slipping off her shoes.

"Alyson, hi." Caleb slid onto a chair beside her.

"Caleb," Alyson said, surprised to see him. "I didn't know if you'd make it after everything that's happened."

"Are you kidding? I was in charge of the decorations. There's no way I was missing this after all the work I've put in."

"The gym looks spectacular. Really."

"I noticed you were here with Devon, but I just wanted to thank you again for everything you did for me. I still can't believe it. It feels like I'm in some dream and any moment now I'm going to wake up."

"Are you okay? It's a lot to take in. Not just the money, but to have your whole family history rewritten."

"Honestly, I don't think everything has sunk in yet, but my mom and I talked all afternoon and I think we're starting to get a little focus." Caleb leaned forward onto his arms, complete exhaustion evident on his face. "I still don't know everything that's going to happen here," Caleb added. "My mom and I have a meeting with an attorney who's going to represent us. There may be a lot of legal stuff to deal with. I guess all I know for sure is that the next few weeks are going to be intense."

"Probably," Alyson agreed. "But hey, until you sort through everything, you still have all of this." She swept her arm around the gym. "Maybe we could hang out sometime."

"I'd like that. I guess the only cloud on my silver lining is that I still don't know for certain what happened to my dad. The cops were certain he killed himself, but my mom and I have maintained from the beginning that he didn't. With everything that has happened in the past twenty-four hours, I'm even more convinced."

"Do you know why the cops were so certain he'd committed suicide?"

"I guess he showed all the typical symptoms. He'd been stressed and depressed after finding a box of his mother's stuff in the attic. He seemed paranoid and secretive in his last days. He wouldn't even talk to my mom about it. The cops said that being depressed and secretive were definite signs of suicidal behavior."

"Did you ever figure out what was on his mind?"

"Not really. I looked for the box of stuff he'd found after he died. It had a bunch of photos, old newspaper clippings, and a key to a lockbox. There didn't appear to be anything obvious that would affect his mood."

"Did you ever check out the lockbox?" Alyson asked.

"No. I guess at some point I decided to let the whole thing go as best I could. I didn't want to upset my mom further by pursuing the murder angle."

"Do you have a box number?" Alyson asked.

"It's on the key."

"The bank is closed tomorrow, but I think you should check it out. I'd be more than happy to help. Are you free after school on Monday?"

"I can be."

"Okay, meet me in front of the main entrance. Maybe we'll find the clue we need to figure out why your dad was so upset in the lockbox."

Caleb stood up. "I'd better get back to my date. She's starting to look a little upset. Oh, I forgot to tell you." He paused before he walked away. "My mom and I want you to keep everything you found in the house. It really belongs to you. It was there when you bought the place."

"Thanks, but we couldn't. It's your heritage."

"We really have nothing to do with any of it. We want you to have it. And there's no reason to sell it. We certainly don't need the money."

"Well," Alyson hedged, "if you really don't want it, my mom and I talked about donating it to the Cutter's Cove Historical Society if we never found an heir. There are a lot of things that not only represent the history of the Cutter family but the history of the town."

"That's a great idea," Caleb said. "Let's talk more about it when we meet on Monday."

Devon walked over and set two glasses of punch on the table as Caleb stepped away. "I didn't want to interrupt. How's he doing?"

"Totally wigging out, I think, but he'll be okay. It's a lot to deal with."

"How much money do you think he inherited?"

"I don't know. I don't think he knows. Must be a lot, though, to prompt someone like Steven Laslow to go all ballistic over it."

"Yeah, that was pretty intense. I'm glad you're okay."

"Thanks to Tucker. I don't know what would have happened if he hadn't been there. I'm seriously thinking about taking him everywhere I go from now on."

"I'm surprised you didn't bring him tonight."

"I might have, if I thought I could get away with it."

Chapter 14

At school on Monday, the gang gathered at their usual table in the cafeteria. It was a warm, sunny day, and they were making plans to go to the beach the following weekend when Caleb hurried over and sat down. "You'll never guess what I found."

"What?" Mac asked.

"After I got home on Saturday night I decided to take another look at the stuff in the attic and found this," Caleb held out a small black journal.

"What is it?" Mac asked.

"A diary of sorts left by Mary."

"Wow, really? What does it say?"

"The diary covers roughly a year's time. The first entry was on the day my dad was born and the last was on the day she married Michael Wellington. The most interesting entries are the ones around the time of her marriage, but I wanted to read you a couple of others. It's really given me some insight into the situation. The first entry was dated August 10, 1955."

Jonathan was born today. He is so beautiful. I never knew I could feel such a deep and pure love. When I look at him I am filled with the certainty that I would do anything for this beautiful child. I think his arrival has affected Barkley too. He tries to act indifferently to the tiny baby who has his eyes, but I can see the softening of his face whenever he looks at him. The delivery was difficult. Barkley thought it best we kept the baby's birth a secret, so I delivered at home. I know Barkley wants to send us away. He says it's for our own good, but I don't agree. I have a year to change his mind.

"There's an entry a day for a year," Caleb informed the group. "There's one toward the middle I wanted to share."

I woke up late this morning after a restless night's sleep. I hurried to the nursery, sure that poor Jonathan would be screaming his head off. I found him changed and fed and playing a game with Barkley that only the two of them seemed to understand. I watched them unnoticed for quite a while. When Barkley lets his defenses down his face glows. After seeing them together my heart is filled with hope. I am certain he won't send us away at the end of the year, as our original agreement dictates.

"Oh my God. That's so beautiful and so sad." Alyson wiped a tear from her cheek.

"There are a lot of other entries that really touched me, but the most relevant ones seem to be just prior to Mary's marriage to Michael."

Barkley is insisting we follow through with our agreement for me to marry an old friend of his, Michael Wellington. I hoped his love for Jonathan would soften him and allow us to live as a family. I've tried to make our relationship work. I truly love Barkley, and I want Jonathan to know his father, but I grow weary of the secrecy and isolation. I have given it much thought, and though it breaks my heart, marrying Michael and giving Jonathan a legal name is the right thing to do for my son. Tomorrow I will marry this stranger and leave the home I have known for the past year, never to return. I am concerned about this arrangement, but it's what Barkley wants. It pains me that Jonathan will never bear the Cutter name. After everything that has happened, maybe it is for the best.

"There's more," Caleb shared.

Today I married Michael Wellington. It was a brief ceremony with only Barkley, Michael, myself, and the minister present. It is my wedding night and I am alone in a strange house with only my son. Michael said his brief vows, signed the marriage and birth certificates, and then left abruptly. I doubt I'll see him again. It has been arranged that our marriage will be dissolved in one year's time. As I sit alone, I have to wonder why Mr. Wellington agreed to go through with this farce. The two men did not seem particularly close. In fact, there was measurable tension between them. Why would Mr. Wellington tie himself to a woman he does not know for a whole year as a favor to a man he clearly has no fond feelings for?

"I'm not sure that helps us to identify my dad's killer, but I thought you all would be interested in the story."

"We are. Thanks for sharing." Alyson placed her hand over Caleb's.

"We still on for the bank?"

"I'll meet you after school."

The rest of the day was endless for Alyson as she feigned interest in the basketball game she participated in during PE and the word-processing document she completed during computer lab. As soon as the final bell for the day rang, Alyson hurried over to the benches in the front of the school, where they had agreed to meet. Trevor and Eli had football practice, so it was just Alyson, Caleb, and Mac that headed to the bank.

As it turned out, the bank president was away on a fishing trip, but the head cashier, Mrs. Partridge, had heard about Caleb's inheritance and was willing to allow him access to the box, provided he had the key. After accessing the box, Caleb pulled out an official-looking document.

"It's Barkley's will. It leaves his entire estate and the Cutter fortune to Jonathan Wellington."

"I wonder why Barkley never told Jonathan about the will," Alyson said.

"Maybe Mary knew," Mac speculated. "She did, after all, have the key to the lockbox. After Mary's death, Steven Laslow must have realized that there was no one who knew about the will other than Barkley, and for whatever reason, he hadn't made any effort to contact Jonathan. As the years went by and no one accessed the lockbox, Laslow must have thought he could embezzle the Cutter fortune and no one would be the wiser. Then Caleb's dad found the key among Mary's things, went to the bank to see what was in the lockbox, and discovered his true heritage. At that point he became a threat."

"How do we know my dad even checked out the lockbox?" Caleb asked.

"I wonder if they keep a record of who's accessed each box and when," Alyson mused. "Let's see if the cashier can help us."

Mrs. Partridge informed them that a log was indeed kept. After checking the computer files she told them that Jonathan Wellington had accessed the box on July 21, 2002; prior to that, no one had accessed it since it was originally opened in August of 1956.

"My dad was here the day before he was killed," Caleb whispered.

"So we have a motive, but how do we trace it back to a murderer?" Alyson asked. "Unless Steven Laslow will admit to doing it."

"Let's take the will and get out of here," Mac said. "If there's an inside person at the bank we might be being watched right now."

They headed to the school library to continue their discussion. Luckily, it was as empty as it always seemed to be.

"What now?" Mac asked.

"Someone must have known that Jonathan had found the will," Alyson began. "As far as we know, the only people who might have known that Jonathan accessed the box are bank employees. Do you think he would have told anyone else?"

"He didn't even tell me or my mom," Caleb reminded them.

"Okay, so assuming that bank employees are the only people who knew, unless Steven Laslow really is guilty, someone at the bank must be the murderer," Alyson deduced.

"I feel like all the evidence we need to figure this out is right in front of us. We just have to put it all together," Caleb said.

"Okay, let's start at the beginning," Mac said with a sigh. "The guys should be done with practice soon. I'll see if they can meet us to help work through the details. The library is going to close soon; we should meet somewhere else."

"I'm starving. Let's head over to Pirates Pizza," Caleb suggested.

"I'll tell the guys to meet us there when they're done." Mac got up and gathered her stuff. "I have my own car, so I'll meet you guys there. You can go on ahead and get a table."

"Now that you've inherited all that money, you can get yourself a car of your own," Alyson said as Caleb climbed into the passenger seat of her Jeep.

"Yeah, maybe I will. Everything has happened so fast. It's hard to get my head around it."

"Give yourself time," Alyson counseled. "A lot has happened in a very short amount of time. It's going to take some getting used to."

Mac joined Alyson and Caleb at Pirates Pizza a few minutes later. Trevor wandered in alone not long after that.

"Eli called home," Trevor explained. "He and Devon have a command performance for dinner because one of their old family friends showed up for a visit. Eli said he'd call when they were done, probably around eight."

"Okay, then it's just us." Alyson pulled a yellow legal pad out of her backpack. "Let's order, then we can get started."

They ordered an extralarge Pirates combo, four salad bars, and a pitcher of soda.

"Now, where do we start?" Mac asked.

"Let's just walk through what we know from the beginning," Alyson suggested.

"The very first thing that happened is that someone broke into Alyson's house," Trevor pointed out. "It coincidentally happened the night after we first started sorting through the contents of the attic. If someone suspected there was incriminating evidence in the house why not break in sooner? Possibly even before Alyson and her mom moved in?"

"Because the attic door was rusted shut," Alyson realized. "I only managed to get it open the night before my first day of school."

"So who knew it was open?" Trevor asked.

"Well, all of us, Eli, my mom, and Chelsea."

"Maybe it was Chelsea who broke in." Mac gasped.

"It couldn't have been Chelsea." Trevor drummed his fingers on the table. "There must be someone else who knew."

"Well, the guy who fixed the stairs," Alyson added. "They were all rotted out, so my mom had them rebuilt."

"Who fixed the stairs?" Mac asked.

"My mom hired a contractor who was referred to her by the manager at Cutter's Cove Market. I guess it was some friend of his. She asked him for a referral because he sold home repair supplies."

"So assuming it wasn't any of us or Chelsea, let's write down the contractor and the store manager as possible suspects," Mac said. "What next?"

"I guess the next thing that happened was the threatening note someone left for Alyson at the diner," Trevor continued.

"Threatening note?" Caleb asked.

"After we first interviewed Ben Wilson we stopped to have a bite to eat, and while we were at there, the waitress handed Alyson a note a man had asked him to give her. It warned her to back off and mind her own business."

"So someone must have known you were snooping around at that point," Caleb pointed out.

"We'd just started," Trevor answered. "In fact, our trip to talk to the folks in town was really our first attempt at tracking you down."

"Other than Ben, who else did you talk to that night?" Caleb asked.

"The clerk at Cutter's Cove Market. She's the one who told us to talk to Ben when we asked about Mary. What was her name?" Alyson asked.

"Gladys," Trevor filled in for her.

"Let's add her to the list," Caleb said. "That makes two connections to Cutter's Cove Market."

"So what's next?" Mac asked.

"We found the bank records, which suggested that Steven Laslow and/or Jason Mastin was embezzling from the Cutter Trust," Alyson added.

"And let's not forget that Steven Laslow tried to kill me," Caleb reminded them.

"Which pretty much implicates Steven as the embezzler," Alyson confirmed.

"How do you suppose he even found out about me, or that you'd figured out who I was?" Caleb asked. "Who else did you talk to?"

"Well, there was Stella Townsend," Alyson remembered. "But she can't be the murderer. She really seemed to want what was best for Caleb. Steven Laslow probably knew about the will. Once we started asking around about Mary and a possible child, someone must have tipped him off that we were looking for an heir. Still, that doesn't explain how he knew the heir was you unless he already knew."

"My father was killed the day after opening the lockbox. Someone at the bank has to have been involved in some way," Caleb pointed out.

"Probably the bank president," Trevor commented.

"Fishing," Alyson exclaimed. "When we went to check the lockbox they told us the bank president was fishing. When we talked to the clerk at the market she said the owner was fishing. I know a lot of people fish so I might be reaching, but maybe they're friends. If so, maybe they're in on it together."

"Okay, so we might have a link between the store and the bank," Trevor said.

"Wait a minute." Alyson sat forward abruptly. "You said your father died of a drug overdose. The drugs had to have come from somewhere. The market has a pharmacy in the back; I noticed it when I was waiting for you to talk to Gladys."

"Yeah, that fits," Caleb said excitedly. "My dad was found at home in his easy chair with the suicide note and empty bottles of sleeping pills and painkillers. The thing is, neither my mom nor I knew he was taking either one. Maybe someone slipped him the drugs, then set the scene to look like a suicide."

"Okay, this is what we know," Alyson summarized, "Devon said there were two sets of prints on the suicide note. One was your mothers," she glanced at Caleb, "and the other set was unidentified. If we assume that the prints belong to the person who killed your dad we just need to match the prints to the four suspects we've identified: Steven Laslow, the trust administrator, probable embezzler, and attempted murderer of Caleb; Jason Mastin, suspected accomplice of Steven's, president of Heritage Industries, and vice president of the bank where the embezzlement trail began; the president of the local bank; and Mr. Sheldon, the store owner. Steven is in custody, so they have his prints, and as banking executives, I'm sure Mastin's and Owen's prints are on file."

"So we just need something with the storeowner's fingerprints," Trevor proclaimed.

"Trevor and I will go to the market and talk the clerk into letting us into the storeowner's office. Trevor can distract her and I'll nab something off his desk," Alyson suggested.

"The pizza's here," Mac informed them. "Let's eat quickly, then we'll all go. Caleb and I can wait in the car."

After they ate they headed over to the store, hoping the same clerk would be working that night. Luckily, she was, along with another woman. She quickly closed her checkstand when she saw Trevor walk in and hurried to greet him.

"You're back. Was Mr. Wilson helpful?"

"Yes, very." Trevor flashed her his biggest smile. "Thank you for the lead."

"Mr. Sheldon stopped in after you left, and I mentioned you wanted to talk to him about an old employee of his. He said he'd catch up with you when he gets back from his trip."

Alyson looked meaningfully at Trevor. "Did he say when he'd be back?"

"No, it depends on how the fishing is going. He's quite the fisherman and can be quite single-minded. He has the county record for catching the largest fish in Spooner Lake. He has a huge picture of it in his office."

"Really? We'd love to see it." Trevor placed an arm around the clerk. "I for one am a fan of fishing myself."

"Sure; follow me."

Gladys unlocked Mr. Sheldon's office door and led them inside. Behind the desk was a huge picture that took up nearly the whole wall. Trevor walked around for a closer look, while Alyson stayed behind and looked for something small that no one would miss but was sure to provide clean prints. She settled on a letter opener, sliding it carefully into her coat pocket.

"Thank you so much for showing us the photo." Alyson started toward the door as a signal for Trevor. "It's really quite something."

"Yes, we should be going now." Trevor turned to follow Alyson.

"What did you come in for?" Gladys asked, confused.

"Oh, the milk for my mom. I completely forgot with all the excitement over the fish," Alyson covered. "Let's not forget the milk, Trev."

"I'll get it for you. Meet me at checkstand four," Gladys offered.

Alyson paid for the milk and she and Trevor returned to the car and filled the others in.

"Eli called while you were inside. I told him what you were doing. He said if you managed to get something from the storeowner's office he'd have Devon call his contact at the police station about getting the prints lifted. He also said that they checked Steven Laslow's prints against the ones on the note and they weren't a match."

"So hopefully either Mastin's or the store managers will be." Caleb sighed.

"Go ahead and call Eli," Alyson instructed.

Mac dialed the number and spoke to Eli. "Eli's going to talk to Devon, then call us back," she said after she hung up. "We should probably go, though. It will seem suspicious if we just sit out here in the parking lot. The clerk might be watching us."

Fifteen minutes later, Devon called to tell them to meet him at the police station. The detective he had talked with before was willing to come in to have the letter opener dusted for prints.

"It looks like there's a good print on the handle," he informed them. "Did you touch it when you picked the letter opener up?" he asked Alyson.

"No, I picked it up by the tip. The print on the handle shouldn't be mine."

"Okay, let's see if it matches any of the prints on the suicide note."

The seconds ticked away, seeming like hours, as the detective studied the prints and the suicide note. Alyson grabbed Caleb's hand in support and held on tightly. Neither of them dared breathe.

"We have a match."

Chapter 15

The next day the gang gathered at their usual table for lunch with the addition of Caleb, who wanted to thank everyone for their help in finding his father's murderer.

"There you are," Chelsea said as she sat down next to Caleb. "I've been looking for you all week. Seriously, if you're not going to be where you're supposed to be you should tell a person. I thought we were going to talk cars. And clothes. I've been giving the matter a lot of thought. As the richest person in Cutter's Cove, you have an image to uphold."

"We were going to talk cars and clothes?" Caleb looked confused.

"Of course we were, silly. Who better to counsel you in your transformation from the D list to the A list?"

"D list?"

"I forgive you for ignoring me for the past few days. We can go shopping after school. I have a list of everything you'll need."

"I'm sorry, but I have plans after school. Drama club," Caleb informed Chelsea.

"Seriously? Now that you're rich, you're going to have to prioritize a little better. Hanging with those drama geeks is only going to lead to your downward mobility. Stick with me and you'll rule the school."

"I think for now I'll stick with my D-list status. Thanks for your offer to help, though. I'll keep it in mind if I ever decide to rule the world."

"Whatever. I have to go." Chelsea got up from her chair. "Let me know when you're ready to join the elite. In the meantime, I guess we can still date. Who knows, maybe I'll rub off on you."

"Wow, she's really . . ." Caleb hesitated as he searched for the right word as Chelsea sauntered away.

"I'm right there with you," Trevor agreed.

"Anyway," Caleb continued, "I really wanted to thank you all for your help in finding my father's killer. Mr. Sheldon is in jail, being held for my father's murder, and Jason Mastin and the bank president are both being questioned about their suspected part in the embezzlement."

"I get why the bank president was involved; money is a big motivator. But why do you think Mr. Sheldon was involved? Was he being paid off by the others?" Mac asked.

"Maybe. The detective investigating the case told me Mr. Sheldon was romantically involved with Mary prior to her affair with Barkley. His motive might have been old-fashioned jealousy and revenge. His good friend, the bank president, asked him to help out, he already held a grudge, so it might have been an easy segue from upstanding citizen to murderer," Caleb guessed.

"I'm sure it'll all come out in the trial," Trevor said.

"The police told my mom that they're going to take a look at Barkley's death as well. He was an old man and it appeared that he died of natural causes, but given the timing of his death in relation to my dad's, they suspect there could be more to it."

"It's been quite a couple of weeks," Trevor commented. "I'm glad it's over."

"I hear you. I'm up for some fun. How about we all go to the Cannery tonight?" Alyson suggested. "I have this radical new dress."

"I'm in," Trevor agreed.

"My treat," Caleb offered.

"Did you see Chelsea's hair?" Mac asked Alyson as they gathered their books to head to their fifth-period classes. "I mean, who does she think she is?"

"I know what you mean. And what about Renee Owens's new look? I mean really. Who would think that was a good idea?"

"So," Alyson said to Mac as they broke off from the rest of the group. "I'm picking up on sparks between you and Eli. Any datelike activity planned for the future?"

"I don't know about dating per se. But when I mentioned the haunted hayride that's coming up next month he said it sounded like fun. I know that's not really a commitment, but there was a definite hint of togetherness in his voice."

"That's great, Mac. I have a feeling Eli's really into you. I think he's kind of shy."

"Shy? You really think so?"

"Yeah I really do. Just be patient. Maybe you should ask *him* out. Something casual, like bowling or pizza."

"Bowling?"

"Some people like bowling."

"Maybe we could ask Eli and Devon out for pizza. Then it wouldn't really be a date."

"I guess that would be okay," Mac agreed.

"What is the haunted hayride anyway?" Alyson asked.

"Every Halloween the drama club puts on this really spooky event. Everyone meets at Jordan's field, near the gate to the dirt road leading up into Black Canyon. Farmers in the area donate hay wagons for the night, and there's this really spooky ride to the Thomases's old barn. There's narration along the way, and the drama kids dress up as ghosts and stuff and jump out at you from the woods as the story unfolds. I mean, everyone knows it's really Ronnie Fisher on his dad's big black stallion under the headless horseman costume, but it feels real at the moment. Anyway, the hayride ends at the old barn and there's a big party, complete with spooky decorations and food."

"Sounds like fun. We should totally go."

Amanda Parker attending something as corny as a haunted hayride. Who would have thought?

Books by Kathi Daley

Come for the murder, stay for the romance.

Buy them on Amazon today.

Zoe Donovan Cozy Mystery:

Halloween Hijinks
The Trouble With Turkeys
Christmas Crazy
Cupid's Curse
Big Bunny Bump-off
Beach Blanket Barbie
Maui Madness
Derby Divas
Haunted Hamlet
Turkeys, Tuxes, and Tabbies
Christmas Cozy
Alaskan Alliance
Matrimony Meltdown – April 2015
Soul Surrender – May 2015
Heavenly Honeymoon – June 2015

Zoe Donovan Cookbook

Ashton Falls Cozy Cookbook

Paradise Lake Cozy Mystery:

Pumpkins in Paradise
Snowmen in Paradise
Bikinis in Paradise
Christmas in Paradise
Puppies in Paradise

Whales and Tails Cozy Mystery:

Romeow and Juliet
The Mad Catter
Grimm's Furry Tail – March 2015

Road to Christmas Romance:

Road to Christmas Past

Cutter's Cove Teen Cozy Mystery Series:

The Secret
The Curse – May 2015
The Relic – July 2015

Kathi Daley lives with her husband, kids, grandkids, and Bernese mountain dogs in beautiful Lake Tahoe. When she isn't writing, she likes to read (preferably at the beach or by the fire), cook (preferably something with chocolate or cheese), and garden (planting and planning, not weeding). She also enjoys spending time on the water when she's not hiking, biking, or snowshoeing the miles of desolate trails surrounding her home.

Kathi uses the mountain setting in which she lives, along with the animals (wild and domestic) that share her home, as inspiration for her cozy mysteries.

Stay up to date with her newsletter, *The Daley Weekly*. There's a link to sign up on both her Facebook page and her website, or you can access the sign-in sheet at: http://eepurl.com/NRPDf

Visit Kathi:

Facebook at Kathi Daley Books,
www.facebook.com/kathidaleybooks

Facebook at Kathi Daley Teen -
www.facebook.com/kathidaleyteen

Kathi Daley Books Group Page –
https://www.facebook.com/groups/569578823146850/

Kathi Daley Birthday Club -
https://www.facebook.com/groups/1040638412628912/

Kathi Daley Recipe Exchange -
https://www.facebook.com/groups/752806778126428/

Webpage - www.kathidaley.com

E-mail - kathidaley@kathidaley.com

Recipe Submission E-mail –
kathidaleyrecipes@kathidaley.com

Goodreads:
https://www.goodreads.com/author/show/7278377.
Kathi_Daley

Twitter at Kathi Daley@kathidaley - https://twitter.com/kathidaley

Tumblr - http://kathidaleybooks.tumblr.com/

Amazon Author Page - http://www.amazon.com/Kathi-Daley/e/B00F3BOX4K/ref=sr_tc_2_0?qid=141823 7358&sr=8-2-ent

Pinterest - http://www.pinterest.com/kathidaley/

CPSIA information can be obtained
at www.ICGtesting.com
Printed in the USA
LVOW11s2348180218
567083LV00019B/350/P